Escape From Gehenna

by Bradley J. Knefelkamp

Deep in the mines of Tartrus, the young were forced to dig ore for the iron weapons of the kingdom of Gehenna – until an incredible thing happened...

ISBN–13: 978-1479381340

Dedicated to Logan, Spencer, and Brielle.
You grew up way too fast.

To Lacie and Milo,
I may have started this book for the other kids,
but I finished it for you.

To Michelle,
Thanks for letting me get distracted.

And in memory of Logan.

HAMAR
MT. ADAMAN
OUTPOST
RUINS OF ASHER
BORBOROS
BOTTOMLESS BOG
SEA OF LYPHE
NORTH FOREST
GEHENNA
MINES OF TARTRUS
CITY OF GEHENNA
PISHON RIVER

Table of Contents

Introduction: The Page	5
One: The Find	8
Two: The Past	15
Three: The Escape	29
Four: The North Forest	43
Five: Hunted	56
Six: The Promise	67
Seven: The Village	76
Eight: The Meeting	84
Nine: A Guide	96
Ten: Followed	111
Eleven: Trapped	120
Twelve: Abandoned	133
Thirteen: The Rescue	141
Fourteen: Buried Alive	151
Fifteen: Forty-Four Riders	162
Sixteen: The Fall	174
Seventeen: Surrender	187
Eighteen: The King	193
Nineteen: A Choice	206
The End...	216

Introduction

THE PAGE

I come from a long line of historians. And, since history has been the passion of my family for three generations, I am determined to carry it on to the fourth. So, years ago, when given the privilege of going through my grandfather's library, I jumped at the opportunity. It was there he kept his favorite and rarest finds. Many were clouded by ages of ambiguity and in need of further validation from outside sources – in other words, myths, folklores, and legends.

The smells of aging paper and pipe tobacco filled the air as I made my way inside the study, and to me, it was like stepping onto hallowed ground. My siblings and I were never allowed into this room when we were young, for the obvious reason that it was a place of serious business, not tomfoolery. I walked in slowly and took in the sight.

Unorganized to the untrained eye, which is everyone's except grandfather's, I scavenged my way through teetering stacks of papers around the sizeable dark walnut desk, as well as bookshelves filled to overflowing with scrolls, loose pages, and countless volumes of books. I could feel the intense study over minute details and fitting together misplaced pieces of the past still lingering in the air.

In this clutter, I came across a particularly fascinating piece of parchment. Its runic inscription, written in a Pre-Saxon dialect, dated it sometime between 450 and 700 AD. Roughly translated it read as follows:

> *"Forty feet beneath Gehenna, and near the northernmost banks of the Pishon River, which runs through that land, lay Tartrus. Hated by all who lived in that region, Tartrus was a mine for iron and a prison for the young. It was there that wills were not merely broken but crushed into dust never to be remade. Torches strained to illuminate its halls and tunnels. But mere flames could not permeate its darkness, for gloom and deep shadow dwelt there, leaving room for nothing else, save the sound of picks against stone. This echoed continuously, interrupted only by the cracking of whips across the backs of the young."*

The paper was brittle, and the iron gall ink showed considerable signs of fading. And, since its theme was brief, I grabbed some stationery from Grandfather's desk and wrote it down to examine its contents at a later time without again disturbing the frail original. When I told Grandfather of the piece, he proceeded to tell me the fascinating tale, or as he insisted calling it, the "history" of Gehenna.

He said he had devoted years to uncovering this obscure legend but put it aside long ago when called upon to research of a sect of people called the Essenes and their connection with the then newly discovered Dead Sea Scrolls. Of course, Gehenna's history got pushed back into the dusty corners of grandfather's library in much the same way it was designated to the recesses of his mind.

Other histories needed research, and grandfather's work on Gehenna was left on a back shelf where I found it.

We spent many weekends together over the next several months poring over all the documents he had uncovered earlier on the topic. Most of them were transcribed from oral traditions, which had been documented centuries later, yet with absorbing detail.

Watching Grandfather dig back in with the renewed passion of his youth made me realize just how much I admired the man. Written down here is the account we unveiled. I have taken the liberty to present it in story form, using the order of events as they were uncovered. While filling in details with possibilities in much the same manner as its oral tradition.

I am sad to say that Grandfather passed away a short time after we completed our research. So, I share the tale with you now in loving memory of him.

The Author

One

The Find

His pickaxe stuck out from the tunnel wall, daring someone strong enough to set it free. Chanse looked at it dumbfounded. Every cell in his body ached from years of non-stop labor in the mine, and the meager rations of often-moldy food left him too thin and weak to have swung it that hard.

Glaring at the ax, the black hand of hatred dug deeper, tearing away at any hope he had left. Every waking minute in the mines meant pain, hunger, and ultimately despair. That was their goal, and he didn't want to let them win – he wouldn't. Lifting his unwilling arm, he grabbed the handle, smooth and well-worn by his own calloused hands, and let go of the bitterness. He really didn't have the strength to set the ax free, but he had the willpower – one more pull. Prying hard, his knuckles whitened, and his face turned red.

"It…is…stuck!" His words came out in grunts from between gritted teeth.

From across the corridor, a boy named Drake walked over and nudged him aside. Grabbing the ax with one hand, he gave it a quick jerk. It didn't budge.

"See." Chanse folded his arms across his chest.

Drake gripped it again, this time with both hands. He placed a sandaled foot up against the carved rock wall and used his body's full weight for leverage. Still, it refused to give.

He stood back, looking at it quizzically as he wiped sweat from the back of his neck, then reached for it again. "Come on," he said. "Just 'cause I'm helping doesn't mean you can just stand there."

Chanse took hold of the handle next to his friend, and together they tugged.

Slaves rarely offered friendship in the mines. Those who became too close were soon separated because their taskmasters, the Batrauks, loved strife. It was their tool of choice for control, and they did all within their power to preserve it. As a way around this tactic, some slaves would stage fights whenever Batrauks were in sight. Chanse learned this the hard way.

On their first day in the mine, he and his twin sister were sent to a small tunnel. She was given the chore of emptying the ore cart while he and another boy dug. Chanse kept his mouth shut, picked up an ax, and started swinging. When the Batrauk left, the boy next to him spoke.

"You new here?"

Chanse nodded. "First day."

"Happy birthday," the boy said, then swung his ax at the wall as if he were trying to kill it.

Chanse could see the anger that the boy directed through the tool he wielded and how he harnessed it as his source of strength. Impressed and feeling somehow challenged, Chanse joined in punishing the mine. He attacked the rock alongside the boy, and it felt strangely good. An unexpected smile appeared on his face until the Batrauk came back. That's when the boy slammed Chanse hard against the tunnel wall. Taken by surprise, Chanse didn't cower or cry but reciprocated with a shove. The scuffle ended with the other boy on top and Chanse beneath him with a fat lip.

The Batrauk, satisfied with the arrangement, left, and the boy got up with a smile.

"You catch on quick," he said. "I'm Drake."

Chanse dabbed a trickle of blood off his swollen lip and sat up. Again, to his surprise, the boy's hand reached out to help him.

As Drake pulled him to his feet, Chanse slugged him hard in the shoulder.

"Hey! What was that for? The show's over." Drake looked at him, confused.

Chanse cocked his head, and a knowing grin slid across Drake's face.

"I only fight when Batrauks are in sight. Even then, only if I think you're worth being around. If they think we hate each other, they make sure we stay together." Drake rubbed his sore shoulder and let out a painful laugh. "You're only the second one to ever push back."

With a nod, he introduced himself as Chanse – just Chanse. Generations of slavery made last names obsolete and all but forgotten. Chanse, however, knew his and knew to keep it secret. The only one he ever told was his sister, and he reminded her of it every day. For him, their family name meant they belonged somewhere and to someone – and that gave him strength.

But, neither Drake's anger nor Chanse's last name gave them enough strength to pry the pickaxe from the mine wall. Together, they let it go, exhausted from their efforts to free it. Chanse leaned against the wall, blackened with mold from the water that trickled in. It filled the air with a pungent stench making it hard for them to catch their breath.

"Stupid thing." He gave the handle a kick, and it budged.

"Yes!" Drake smiled, seeing it move.

They both grabbed hold and once more gave a quick, strong tug. It dislodged and left a gaping hole, a dark window into a mysterious void. Chipping away at rock had always led to more rock, not to empty space. Wind whistled through, and the breeze brushed across their skin.

"Fresh air," Chanse sighed.

He closed his eyes and leaned in, taking deep breaths, drinking it in like water.

Suddenly, chunks of stone sprayed his face. Jerking back, he opened his eyes and saw Drake's pickaxe had come within inches of hitting him. Drake then pulled it back for another swing.

"Hey! Watch it!" The scowl on Chanse's face and the irritated tone in his voice seemed to go unnoticed.

"Come on. Let's make it bigger!" Drake said and swung again. "Don't you want to know what's on the other side?"

Chanse stood back, picked up his ax, and swung. He attacked the hole alongside Drake, matching him swing for swing, until they had created an opening big enough to squeeze through.

Drake threw his pickaxe to the ground and grabbed a torch. Headfirst he squeezed his torso into the tight space, squirming and kicking his way inch by inch.

Chanse picked up another torch and waited for his turn. Being smaller than Drake, he grew impatient. "If you would've let me go first, I'd have been in there by now!" he shouted.

Drake kicked violently as he backed out, his eyes wide with fear.

"Get down!" he yelled, diving into a corner and covering his head with his hands.

Chanse stood confused when a flurry of flying black creatures exploded through the hole. It knocked him back, and he landed on top of Drake. In an instant, they were surrounded by thousands of winged rodents screeching and scratching through the hole in the wall. Some landed on Chanse, crawling along his back, their sharp claws tearing his shirt and puncturing his skin before taking again to flight. Then they escaped into the darkness – a canopy of flapping.

* * * *

The Batrauk closed his eyes and winced, clenching his mouth tightly, not letting out a sound. Pain from the branding would last for hours. He knew that, but this was the honor of becoming a general, one of the few under the direct command of Dymorius. He was lucky; he morphed brown, not grey, and dumb like most.

He opened his eyes. The long red scar ran down his arm from his shoulder to his elbow, and his flesh reeked from being cauterized. He held back the urge to vomit. The pain would stop soon enough. Besides, he had a new role to fulfill.

The officer that administered the hot iron to his flesh grunted. "You took it well enough. Now back to work!"

Stomping over to the door, the new general threw it open, ready to step into his authority. Instead, he walked right into pandemonium. For the first time ever, Batrauks had lost control. The young were running and screaming up and down the corridors as bats infiltrated its tunnels.

"What's happening out here!" His wet, guttural voice rang throughout the hall.

"Ngraauuk...young ones, afraid." A subordinate grey croaked back. "Don't know why."

"Well, get control over this situation or…Mmmff."

A large bat collided with the new general's face, knocking him back over two young slaves that had been crawling away to escape the flapping invasion.

Lifting himself from the ground, he grabbed

a bat in mid-flight and crushed it in his fist. He shook it in the face of the grey and screamed. "Where did these come from?"

"Don't know...ngraauuk. Just appeared and are filling the place." He flinched.

The general turned in anger from brown to a reddish color. His eyes bulged and pulsated. He shoved one of the young out from under him and backhanded his fellow Batrauk, stinging his branded arm.

The grey cowered. Then, grabbing a bat, said, "Young ones are so scared of them. Don't know why. They're delicious." Cramming the rodent into his toothless mouth, he swallowed it whole and laughed. "They tickle," he said, watching its form pushing against the inside of his stomach.

"Enough!" the brown shouted, drool flying from the corners of his mouth in all directions. Gathering subordinate greys as he tromped through the tunnel, he barked out his order. "Follow me. We must find out where this trouble is coming from and stop it!"

"Why?" asked a grey.

Flexing his full authority, the new general grabbed his fellow Batrauk by the throat, promptly and permanently silencing the creature. Turning to the others, he answered, "If bats can get in, *brats* can get out!"

Two

The Past

The rim of the cart felt slippery and warm under Chelly's hand as she pushed against it to stand back up. She had wedged herself between it and the wall when the invasion of bats filled the tunnel. As they disappeared into the darkness, the shrieks of slaves echoing down the corridor became more and more distant.

She wiped the fresh dung off her hands onto her ragged shirt. Then she blew on the cinders of her torch, which had gone out with the rush of wings. It burst back to flame, not so much lighting the corridor as casting deep shadows. Reaching into the cart where Breena had ducked for cover, Chelly touched the girl's back to let her know all was clear.

"Aaauu! Get it off me, get it off me!" the girl screamed, waving her once-lit torch wildly above her head and burning Chelly with its embers.

"Hey, hey, careful, it's me!"

Hearing Chelly's voice, Breena looked up with her large dark eyes, quivered, and began to sob. The youngest and smallest in their crew of five, she worked alongside her brother, Drake, just as Chelly did with Chanse. Batrauks always put siblings together so they could torment one to punish the other.

"Just stay in there," Chelly told her. "Ricker and I will push the cart the rest of the way."

"I didn't agree to that!" Ricker crawled out from underneath, where he had taken shelter.

"Where do you think those things came from?" Chelly said, looking down the tunnel in the direction of Chanse and Drake.

"How should I know?" Ricker brushed himself off.

Chelly pointed her finger down the passageway.

"Yes, I know they came from that way, but I don't know from where – exactly." His last word came out snarky as if she were stupid for pointing.

"We've been digging in the lowest part of the mine ever since you and Drake got caught stealing food." Chelly put her hands on her hips.

"Yeah, don't remind me. There isn't even much ore down there." He leaned against the cart. "How can they still demand that we get just as many cartloads by the end of each shift?"

Chelly rolled her eyes. "The bats came from down there."

"I know. I just said that."

"Down where my brother and your best friends just happen to be," Chelly said, crossing her arms.

Ricker stood motionless, putting the pieces of

Chelly's points together.

"What are you waiting for?" he said at last and grabbed hold of the cart. "Come on, push!"

Chelly smirked, shook her head, and leaned into it next to him. He wasn't a bright boy, she thought, but once he caught on, he was good to have around.

Soon the tunnel filled with the sound of grinding wheels racing toward their destination. When they arrived, Chanse and Drake were still trying to relight a torch.

"Look what we found!" Drake said, touching his torch to their flame and waving it at the empty space in the wall. The hole, now carved even larger by the claws of wings and feet in the mass exodus, whistled with a steady breeze.

"Is that where those things came from?" Chelly asked.

"I was trying to go through when all of a sudden – whoosh!" Drake flailed his arms as he spoke. "They came straight at me!"

"Where do you think it goes?" Ricker asked.

"That's what we're going to find out." Drake neared the entrance and climbed easily through the now broad opening. He looked back with a grin. "This'll be fun," he said, then descended the sloping wall on the other side.

The others followed. Sliding over loose stones and stalagmites, they reached level ground below. Wet guano spotted the otherwise sandy cave floor. The moist air wasn't fresh, but it was better than what they endured in the mine. Chelly felt like she could breathe since the first time she entered them.

"It's huge!" she said, looking up at the high ceiling. As the others spread out in exploration, she wandered over to an obscure mound and bent down to inspect it.

"It can't be." Chelly brought her flame in closer.

"What is it?" Chanse came over and crouched down next to her.

She pulled her long hair back and examined it in disbelief.

"It looks like people lived here! These are pots and things." She reached in and moved some objects around, exposing bugs that lay beneath that quickly scattered.

"Even, bones," Chelly said, jerking back after touching one. She brushed her hand off on her dirty clothes and stood back up. The sound of Drake and Ricker dashing off to explore caught the attention of Chanse, who ran off to join them. The light of their torches grew dim as they all turned a corner, but Chelly didn't recall seeing Breena with them.

"Breena?" Her voice echoed. In the excitement, she didn't notice where the young girl had gone. Looking around, she finally saw her silhouette at the hole they had come through.

"Breena, come in!" she said, making her way up the sloping wall toward her.

The young girl shook her head.

"It's okay, sweetie. We're all in here."

Chelly coaxed her to the ledge, where she sat

with her legs dangling and breathing heavily.

"It's okay, let go. I'm right here," Chelly said in a calm, reassuring voice that reminded her in that moment of her own mother's.

Breena shoved off awkwardly with a high-pitched squeal; and tumbled headlong into Chelly, who took the full brunt of the force. Landing flat on her back, she cascaded down the embankment with Breena on top of her. When the two came to a sudden stop at the bottom, Breena got up quickly, but Chelly couldn't breathe. She rolled onto her side, involuntary groans coming out of her as she tried to inhale.

"Chelly?" Breena reached out to her. "What's wrong?"

The groans gave way to coughing as Chelly got onto her hands and knees.

"Are you all right?" Breena cried softly, her voice as slight and timid as the touch of her small hand resting on Chelly's arm.

Chelly opened her eyes and saw the worried look of her friend.

"I'm fine. I just…" Another cough eked out, followed by a massive gulp of air. "…swallowed wrong." She knelt on the ground, bent over with her hands on her knees until she could finally breathe again. "Why didn't you come in when we all did?"

"This place scares me."

Chelly looked at the frail little girl reaching out her arm to help her up. She took hold and stood. "Well, I'm glad you're here now."

"I don't like it." Breena didn't let go of

Chelly's hand. "But, then I thought about being alone with Batrauks, and that felt worse."

Chelly understood. Everyone hated the taskmasters of the mines. She didn't know what about them repulsed her more. Their oversized eyes, which harbored great, pooling black pupils that morphed into tall, thin slits when they were about to attack. The touch of their skin, smooth and clammy, stretching over their frames like a poorly fitted sheet. Or their awful, toothless mouths. Too wide for their heads, they extended over halfway across their faces and concealed those long, sticky tongues used to lash out and slap the faces of the young, leaving a slime-dripping red welt.

"Well, maybe we won't have to worry about bumping into them in here," Chelly said, putting an arm around her friend.

"But what if we do?" Breena looked back at the hole. "We would be in real trouble. I can't even think of what they'd do to us."

"You'd rather go back into the mine with all the bats?" Chelly asked.

Breena shuddered.

"I can't believe this place!" Drake said, returning with Chanse and Ricker. "Look at all this stuff we found." They dumped everything they had gathered into a mound in front of Chelly and Breena. Ricker laid hold of a knife and strapped it around his waist by his pant cord. Drake picked up a larger blade with a broken tip.

"On guard!" Drake said, challenging Ricker to a duel. The two stood, swinging their weapons wildly into the air at each other.

"Back up before you hit someone with those things," Chanse said as he rummaged through the pile.

As Drake and Ricker sparred off, a glint from something shiny caught Chanse's eye. He reached down and pulled up a round, tarnished piece of metal with a clasp on one side and a hinge on the other. He tried opening it, but corrosion kept it shut.

Breena gasped, trembling as she pulled a book out from the pile. She brushed off the dirt and dung. Flaking letters of gold glimmered across its aged cover in the torchlight.

"You can't read," her brother said, snatching her treasure.

"Give it back!" she screamed and grabbed at it, but Drake's long arm held it out beyond her reach.

He's too rough with her, Chelly thought. *The way he speaks down at her, making her feel smaller and less capable than she is.*

"Give it back to her," Chelly said.

"Our father is a scribe. His job is writing books." Drake held it up to his face as if inspecting its quality. "He would bring home the histories and sometimes read us portions that told of how peaceful this country used to be." His demeanor then changed from boastful to shame. "But then he would rewrite them until they suited Dymorius. And after finishing each one to his approval, our father would hand the original over to be burned so that just the copy remained – just like he handed us over."

"That's not fair!" Breena blurted out. "You

know he hated his job!"

"Sure he did. That's why he did it so dutifully, staying up late into the night reworking the stories while we were left to fend for ourselves."

"He loved us." She looked at the book in her brother's hand as if it were her father.

"Too bad no one here is a reader."

"I am." Chelly held out her hand for the book. She didn't want to admit it but knew she could get the book back into Breena's hand if she did.

Drake looked sideways at her. "Sure you are."

"She is." Chanse stared at Drake to challenge him.

"Here, then." Drake shoved the book into Chelly's hand. "If you're a reader, tell us what it says."

Chelly glared at Drake. Breena sat down beside her as she stuck her torch into the ground and examined the cover. Some of its letters were nearly gone, and it was in cursive, which she always found difficult to decipher.

Unlike most, Chelly learned to read before entering the mines. Her mother started teaching her when she had shown interest at just three years of age. When she began explaining letters and their sounds, Chelly took to it like a bird to flight. She loved to read, a passion she inherited from her mother, just as she had inherited her name – Rachel.

Her mother had a precious book kept hidden beneath the floorboards in the cooking room, so it wouldn't be found during the frequent raids when

Batrauks searched homes for signs of treason. Chelly often wondered what could be so important or dangerous about that book. Mother didn't hide any of the others.

The day they were sent into the mines, she gave Chelly that book. Small with tiny print, each page as thin as a strand of hair. Her mother concealed it in the folds of Chelly's clothing and told her to keep it secret. Just holding it flooded her with memories of her mother; the way she looked and spoke, even the smell of her apron came vividly back as if she were standing there with her.

The book Drake had thrust upon her was nothing like it. Damaged by water and time, its warped pages were written on in blotchy letters,

"It's a diary," Chelly said, flipping through it. She scanned the entries with Breena looking over her shoulder.

"What does it say?" Chanse asked. Chelly just shrugged as she muttered sounds and syllables, skimming lines that were still readable.

"Oh! Okay, here's something," she said. Everyone but Drake huddled around to listen. "It's about Dymorius first coming here to help."

"Help? That can't be right," Ricker said.

Chelly just shrugged. "Here, listen."

"It is more than rumor; Dymorius has come to our aid! He has stood up against the king on our behalf and voiced our..."

She stumbled over the letters.

"...complaints.
No longer will we stand under the rule of a single set of strict laws created by one, etched in stone.
Right and wrong are different for everyone in every circumstance. We will take back our freedom!
We will dictate ourselves!"

Flipping the pages, Chelly found more entries about Dymorius empowering the people. How they stood up for themselves, making declarations in the high courts of not needing a king. They desecrated the places of government and worship, breaking windows, busting down doors, and setting them on fire. She came upon another entry and read it aloud:

"The king is leaving! And taking with him those he calls 'the faithful.'
The 'dependents' we call them.
Leave and never bother trying to re-enter our graces, mindless ones! We know the real reason he leaves, we are too strong. Our wills are like iron. We are free to become whomever we desire. Kings and Princes all!
Hail Dymorius! Our Liberator!"

"This doesn't make any sense!" Chanse exclaimed. "Are they talking about the same Dymorius?"

"Can't be," Ricker said. "Everyone knows

he's the reason we suffer."

"I don't know who else it could be," Chelly said, flipping more pages.

"Doesn't make sense." Drake found a sandy spot on the ground and reclined. "Sounds like some gibberish our father would have written in one of his rewrites." He picked a small rock from under his side and threw it across the cave, where it landed with an echoing thud.

"What else does it say?" Chanse asked.

"The rest is too damaged and faded. I can't read it." Chelly fanned the pages when one of the last ones fell from the book. She picked it up and read it aloud.

'What have we done? We try to escape, to hide, only to be hunted and caught for sport. We long for the days of our king, the days of peace and plenty.
If only he could hear our cry for help and forgive us for our stupidity. If we could, we would flee to his gates. But now it's too late. They are coming for us. We hear their chants of triumph. Our ears are pierced with their squeals of victory.'

She gently replaced the page, closed the diary, and handed it back to Breena's eager grasp.

Breena stashed it into the pouch that hung around her waist. And, pulling tight on its draw chords, she tied it shut with a knot.

"This is our way out!" Drake said, sitting up,

the flames of his torch reflecting in his widening eyes. “This cave has an exit somewhere. We can walk right out of this place.”

“You’re right!” Ricker said, jumping to his feet.

Chanse looked confused. “Out to where? Where are we going to go?”

“Home.” Chelly blurted out.

“Ha! Not me,” Drake’s said as he stood. “Dad handed us over once to this pit, and he’d do it again. I think we should search for wherever that other king and his people went.”

“But if these people couldn’t escape, what makes you think we can?” Breena said. She cradled her pouch to her chest with both arms, curling herself into a ball.

A smile grew on Chanse’s face. “We do have an advantage…”

Chelly looked crossways at him, wondering what he was thinking.

“No one knows we’re missing,” he said with a grin.

Drake bent down, picking anything useful out of the pile. Ricker and Chanse joined him, filling their pouches with knives, lengths of rope, and assorted odds and ends.

“Come on, you two.” Ricker looked over at the girls as he stashed one last item into his already bursting sack. Torches in hand, the boys headed to what appeared to be the main tunnel. Chelly started to follow, but Breena didn’t move. Her eyes glistened with tears in the torchlight.

Chelly grabbed her friend by the hand. "Come on. Let's stick together."

"Hurry up!" Drake hollered, not stopping to wait.

Breena squeezed Chelly's hand harder the further they went.

"Let them stay ahead of us," Chelly whispered. "I don't want to be the first to run into any more bats."

Breena nodded, and a shy smile crossed her face.

Rounding a bend, the tunnel broke off into three narrow passageways that ran like tall cracks in the earth.

"Which one do we take?" Ricker peered down each one, looking for signs of an exit.

"Let's split up and see," Drake said. "You go down that one, Chanse takes the one over there, and I'll…"

"Bad idea," Chanse said, and Chelly knew what would happen next. She had seen them butt heads a hundred times, and Drake always lost the argument, but by brute strength would win the battle. "If we separate, someone could get lost, and then what have we gained?"

"Listen!" Drake raised his voice, walking over to the opening he had chosen for himself, "Do you want to spend all our time…"

"Quiet." Chelly stepped between them with her hand up to her mouth. "I hear something."

"Yeah, you hear loudmouth..." Drake began, but then the noise happened again, this time followed by voices. "They must've come through here!"

All five stood frozen silent. "Batrauks," Chelly whispered, hoping they were looking to seal up the place the bats had come through.

"Ngraauuk. Over there. Torchlight!" the Batrauk's call echoed, then came the familiar sound of pick against stone.

"Stay close," Chanse said, grabbing her hand and pulling her along down one of the tunnels. Before she knew what was happening, they ran in different directions, Ricker into the far tunnel and Drake into the center one. Looking back, she saw Breena left standing alone. She hadn't moved.

"Run!" Chelly yelled back before disappearing behind a bend.

When she saw a light coming up behind them. Chelly pulled back on Chanse's arm and called out for Breena to hurry. The light became brighter.

She must be terrified to be able to run that fast, Chelly thought.

But, instead of her frail friend coming around the corner, Chelly stared straight into the face of a Batrauk.

Though she ran, the flapping of webbed feet drawing closer was always in her ears. A clammy hand reached out, and Chelly felt it brush against her back, almost catching her by the hair. She bolted forward with renewed urgency and passed her brother. Her feet flew as her legs took long, effortless strides as if they weren't even a part of her body. Something else made them run, directing them around each corner and over each stone. Her heart wanted to burst out of her chest to get away from the fire in her lungs.

Just then, Chanse tripped, pulling her down with him. She struggled to get up when something hit hard on the back of her head, then all went black and silent.

Three

The Escape

Incense saturated the room with stale, smoky air, leaving the senses dulled. He stood a moment, taking in the fragrance he had grown to love, drew in a deep breath, and throwing back the curtain, stepped in to take the place of honor on his throne. It was time to feast.

Thirteen candles lit the hall, each on its stand forming a circle around the perimeter of the room. Lines of wax crept down like tentacles and pooled around each base from the long anticipation of the Ruler's entrance. His throng had gathered hours before, their minds now soaked with the intoxicating atmosphere. Prostrate bodies covered the floor, swaying rhythmically to the dissonant melody they chanted. They had melded into a single desire, that of giving him power, for only then could they hope to continue their illusions of ecstasy and freedom.

Dymorius glared out over his subjects, his eyes meeting their glazed expressions. He felt their wills conquered by his own, their strength becoming his, their power entering him as they bowed in fear, adoration, and disdain. He breathed the air deeper still, and his form grew once more to its impressive size, filling out the breastplate he wore. He gorged himself on their worship even as his craving for it grew into an unquenchable desire.

This was his feast, an insatiable gluttony of the senses drawing life from the degradation of others and gaining strength from their weakness. They became less as he became more, sucking them dry while satisfying himself. And each time he set his sights on growing larger.

* * * *

Chanse opened his eyes or at least thought he did. He blinked hard and opened them again, still no light. When he first experienced Tartrus and its darkness it frightened him, but after time it became normal, expected, just a fact of life.

Sitting up, he tried to move but found his left foot entangled. A rope had wrapped around his ankle. He freed himself and followed it on his hands and knees to a pile of stones, feeling his way up the wall of rubble reaching the ceiling.

It puzzled him for a moment.

I must have set off some kind of trap.

Chanse's heart skipped a beat and started back up with a huge thump. Where was Chelly? She must've been lying next to me. He thought he remembered pulling her down. Getting back onto his hands and knees, he reached out into the darkness.

He felt the cold fine sand, the frayed rope, loose stones. Images of his sister lying crushed beneath the rocks raced across his mind and panic set in.

"Chelly?" He tried to yell, but it came out as a raspy whisper. He coughed, cleared his throat, and tried again, but the dust-filled air made it impossible.

He felt along the line of boulders that reached the top of the cave, sealing it completely. There was nothing but dirt and stone. Then his hand brushed against something sticking out from beneath the pile of rubble. Fingers! He recoiled hoping he was wrong, that it was some sort of trick of his imagination. He reached out again, found the cold limp hand, then felt the webbing in between the fingers – a Batrauk.

Relieved, he turned again toward the empty space and searched for his sister. His hands swept along the sandy floor as he crawled until his fingers brushed against the softness of hair. He followed it to her shoulders and shook her gently, hoping she wasn't hurt. She didn't move. Chanse huddled close and listened. She was breathing. He shook her again, still no response. He shook harder.

"Chelly."

Her limp figure stiffened, then stirred.

"Are you hurt?" he said choking on each word.

She wheezed out a quiet, "What happened?"

Between fits of coughing, Chanse explained as much as he had figured out. That the people she read about must have set a trap to protect themselves from anyone trying to get in, which is why the rocks fell behind them. Otherwise, they would have been crushed beneath the rocks.

When Chelly regained her voice, she bombarded him with questions. "How long have I been lying here, and where are the others? Where's Breena? Is there a way out?" she asked without giving him time to answer.

"I don't know."

"What do you mean? You don't know how long we've been here, or where the others are or…"

"I don't know any of it."

Chelly cleared her throat, sniffled, and coughed but didn't say anything.

"Come on," Chanse said. "There's got to be a way out of here." He had Chelly hold onto his pant leg so they wouldn't lose each other as they crawled through the dark on their hands and knees.

Hours passed as they wandered through the cave, scraping knees and crashing headlong into walls, but the slow trudge made it feel like days. A couple of times they thought they saw light, just to find their eyes were playing tricks on them. All the while, darkness pervaded them with an overwhelming sense of hopelessness. Instead of thinking they were on their way toward freedom, Chanse wondered if they weren't entombed.

"Can you see anything?" Chelly tugged his leg.

He stopped and squinted. Faint grey shapes took form, but not with any clarity.

"I'm not sure. I think my eyes are tricking me again."

"I definitely see a dim light," Chelly said.

Chanse blinked. "Where?" He leaned forward and his face met a wall of stone.

"To our left."

He backed up and leaned left, his head hitting another wall.

"I mean right."

"Are you sure this time?"

"What's your problem?"

"Nothing."

Chanse reached out with his hand before changing positions. Around the corner, the blackness did in fact lighten.

"That's got to be a way out," Chanse said, moving on with renewed hope.

The tunnel got smaller the brighter it became and Chanse kept crouching further and further down. The sandy floor gave way to mud and dirt. It leveled the ground leaving a funnel-like tube. Chanse lay down and squirmed his way through the long passage on his belly. Inching his way, the tunnel tightened around his chest until he stopped.

"What's going on? Why'd you stop?" Chelly's muffled voice barely reached his ears.

"It's too small. I can't get through."

"I'll push!"

A moment later he felt her feet push hard against his. The shove wedged him in, and Chanse could hardly breathe.

"Why aren't you moving?"

Chanse couldn't take a breath deep enough to answer. He gulped for air but could only inhale in small shallow pants. Panic made him want to take as deep of a breath as possible, which wedged him tighter.

He exhaled what oxygen he had, thinking, if I let all my air out, I might be able to move a little.

He felt a blow to the bottoms of his feet and skidded forward a couple of inches, leaving some skin from his shoulder behind.

He gasped for breath when she kicked him again. His torso cleared the hole and he pulled himself to the other side.

A moment later Chelly's arm and head appeared in the hole as she wiggled through. He grabbed her hand, pulled, and her smaller frame emerged with ease.

"Thanks for the push."

"Well, you were in ... my ... way."

Chelly's eyes widened.

Chanse turned around to see what she seemed so amazed at. Breaking through a gap near the ceiling, the spray of sunlight lit the floor. A pool of water lay directly below, feeding the tree roots that wound their way down to it from above.

Scurrying over to the pool, Chelly dipped her hand in and lifted some to her lips.

"It's fresh," she said laughing with relief. "Drink some."

Chanse stuck his face in the pool, drawing in great mouthfuls while Chelly continued drinking hand to mouth. For a long time, they sat in the shower of light quenching their thirst.

With his belly full, Chanse set his sights on reaching the opening in the ceiling.

"I'm going up," he said, walking over to where the roots wound thick down the rocky wall. "You coming?"

"In a minute." Chelly dipped her hand in the water and rubbed her face repeatedly.

"Are you ready yet?"

Chelly got up, and Chanse froze. Beneath the years of dirt and ash, she had transformed, and he found himself staring into the face of their mother. Mom. His mouth formed her name without a sound as warm memories played in his mind.

"What's the matter with you?"

Chanse shook the images from his head. "Huh? Nothing."

"Then let's get out of here."

Chanse grabbed a root and climbed with Chelly following close behind.

"Stop. Wait. I'm getting down." Chelly jumped down.

"What's wrong?"

"I'm getting showered with rocks and dirt." She brushed herself off. "I'll climb up when you're out."

It was an easy climb with the help of large outcroppings of rock and strong roots that twisted their way up. Reaching through the hole, Chanse clawed at the soil and sod and pulled himself out.

Sunlight pierced his eyes like daggers, filling them with tears. As his sister's hand emerged he grabbed it, pulling her up to the surface. They buried their faces in their hands letting their eyes adjust.

He felt the soft touch of a breeze, as the sun's

rays reached deep into his skin, warming his bones.

"It feels so good," Chelly said.

"Yeah, I've been cold so long, I forgot I was cold."

As his eyes grew accustomed to the sun, he lowered his hands and blinked away the tears. A vast meadow surrounded them, the grasses bowing to the will of the wind in ever-changing directions. Chanse hadn't remembered colors being so alive. The grasses radiated infinite shades of yellow and gold with splotches of green. Behind them, large trees dotted the hills and stood like lone giants watching over their fields. Above them, the sun hung high in a sky much bluer than he recalled.

Chanse fidgeted with the round metal object he had recovered from the cave, prying and rubbing it between his fingers until flecks of rust fell off. If I could just get this thing open. Defeated, he dropped it back into his pouch and shook the soreness out of his hands.

They wandered the hillsides for much of the afternoon, not knowing where they were or where they were headed when they crested a hill that looked out over a broad valley. Below stood a weathered stable with several horses standing in its shade.

The twins had grown up with an old nag that their father used for pulling their cart into town. A docile animal with a low sagging back and half-blind, Chanse's earliest memories were of holding onto its main, swaying back and forth as it clopped dutifully alongside his father.

These horses were different, the kind he

dreamed of riding when he was young enough to still have dreams, the kind that were in the stories their parents told at night before drifting off to sleep. He saw horses like these for the first time, the day he and his sister turned six – the day they were torn away from their home.

That morning their father had taken him aside and lifted him onto a chair. Eye to eye, he faced his dad and saw the regret that those eyes held.

"You are my son," he said his voice wavering as his grip grew tight around Chanse's shoulders. "Today they will try to change that. They will take you away and blame me for what they do to you. The next time I see you, you'll be as tall as I am… practically a stranger."

Chanse couldn't hear the rest of what his father said. The tears he held back made his ears ring. The next thing he heard were the words, "You are Chanse Adaman. You are my son. I love you. Don't ever forget." And Chanse never did.

The abduction of the young had been taking place in Gehenna for generations. And though their parents had tried to prepare them by teaching them to always trust one another and always be there for each other, they couldn't prepare themselves.

When the Batrauks arrived, their parents dutifully handed them over. They were lifted into a wooden cart with tall iron bars and spikes across the top that curled in and downward.

Two horses left, pulling the wagon down the dirt road, away from their home. Chanse and Chelly looked back. More Batrauks on horses formed a line behind them. Between the rows of Batrauks, they caught a glimpse of their parents. When their mother saw their faces, she screamed. Pain wrenched her face as she broke out of the embrace of their father and ran after them. Chanse remembered Chelly turning away, burying her face in her hands, unable to watch, but he did. And every day since he wished he hadn't.

Three riders turned around and charged at their mother, but their father rushed in and pulled her aside. He saved her from being trampled, but five more dismounted, pounced on them and subdued them. The last vision Chanse had of their mother and father was of them being dragged away in chains.

Later, he heard rumors that adults were sent to an even more terrible place in Gehenna than the mines, a place from which no one ever returned. But he never shared that with his sister.

Remembering that day, his eyes stung hard as tears welled up once more, but this time not from the glare of the sun. He stopped and sat down in the long grass. Chelly sat next to him and buried her head in her shirtsleeve. Chanse turned away and swallowed hard but couldn't choke back all of his tears. Many of them escaped, rolling down his face and landing on the dry, lifeless grass that could not drink them in.

When he could stop his tears, Chanse looked up and saw two clouds drifting through the sky. He lay down and envied the billows that hung over Gehenna, free from its control. They sailed by.

"Look," he said to Chelly, pointing up. "What would it be like to be up there right now?"

Chelly watched as the clouds took on familiar shapes, and soon they were both pointing out things they saw hidden in the ever-changing forms.

"Do you think we should try to find our way home?"

Chelly asked the question that he didn't want to answer. He took a deep breath. "I don't think there is a home for us anymore."

"I have the feeling you're not telling me something that you've known for a long time."

Chanse hesitated and hung his head. He didn't speak, so Chelly did.

"That day they took us, and Mother ran after, I heard the clanking of chains. For a moment I looked back and saw them taken away." Chelly paused, then asked the question, "What do you know?"

Chanse stumbled around with his words trying desperately to find a way to spare her, filling in some, but not all of the missing pieces. He didn't tell her that their parents were most likely in a far worse place, just that they weren't allowed back to their house. As he did she looked away again at the clouds, her expression didn't change, there was no burst of sorrow or grief. Chanse could see that somehow, deep down, she knew it from the very day they were taken.

"I see," she said when he finished, nothing more.

The news needed time to sink in. He got up and walked a bit further on, leaving her there sitting motionless and alone, staring out across the valley. He meandered across the hillside kicking at clods of dirt while his restless mind thought of what they were going to do now. They had escaped, but they weren't free.

* * * *

As Chanse wandered off, Chelly reached into the pouch that hung by its cord around her waist and took out the small book their mother had given her. She looked at the cover, plain brown leather, soft from its years of use. Her mother inherited it from her mother who received it from hers. And so, it passed on for generations.

She opened it and began to read wherever the pages separated. As she did, she sensed her mother's presence, her smell, her touch, and even her embrace. She heard her mother's voice pronouncing each word she read, and the book somehow brought great comfort mixed with sadness. Her mother could touch her, yet she could not touch back.

She read until she felt her fear subside. Closing the small book and placing it back into her pouch, she followed her brother's trail in the tall grass, which lay bent along the hillside where he'd walked, and caught up with him down at the stable.

* * * *

"And what about Breena, Drake, and Ricker?"

It startled Chanse to hear her voice right behind him. He turned to see the brave face of his twin.

"We have to assume the best," he said.

"So, you're saying that they escaped and are on their way to the other kingdom?" She sounded doubtful.

"If it's possible, then maybe we should believe it." Picking up a rock, he turned and threw it hitting the roof of the stable. "Come on," he said. "There's a kingdom to find. And there's our ride."

"The horses?" she asked.

"If we ride them, we'll be able to cover twice as much ground and find our way that much quicker. We may even catch up to the other three."

Chelly stopped and folded her arms in defiance. "We've never even ridden a horse before."

He looked at her and shook his head.

"I mean a real horse. Not that old nag we had."

"What could be so hard about it?" he asked. "We just hop on its back and it goes."

"But we don't know where we're going!" she said.

"True, but there's no quicker way to get away from here," he said walking along the fence line. She followed.

Chanse opened the gate.

"Here, I'll give you a boost," he said and stepped next to a smaller animal.

"You get on first, it's your idea."

"Fine, give me a boost then." He lifted his foot for her to grab.

Pushing off, he laid his arms across the beast,

which moved away to the side. Desperate for something to grab onto, Chanse pawed at the animal as he slid down its sleek, wide, body and fell face-first to the ground. Chelly turned away and covered her mouth to hide the smirk on her face, but the horse whinnied at him in defiant laughter.

"Real funny," Chanse said picking himself up off the ground.

Chelly turned toward the gate. "Come on, let's get walking."

"Wait! I have an idea." Chanse rushed out before her.

Behind the stables, Chanse climbed a fence attached to the back wall and pulled himself onto its thatched roof. It surprised him to see Chelly follow. When they had crossed to the other side, they could see all the horses just below them. Chanse walked over and stood above the tallest one. Black as Tartrus, it had a long mane that flowed down on one side of its neck.

"Are you crazy?" Chelly raised her voice.

"Look, all we have to do is lower ourselves and..."

"You are crazy!" she said.

"I picked the tallest one, so it won't be so far. Come on."

Chelly stood there, her head shaking in disapproval. Chanse looked down again at the horse. The drop didn't seem too far.

"Jump!" Chelly yelled pulling him off of the stable and jumping with him.

They landed on the horse with Chelly in front

gathering fistfuls of its mane and Chanse holding tightly to her shirt. The spooked animal bolted through the open gate and tore across the meadow.

"Whaja…d'that…for?" Chanse said, grappling for a better grip around his sister's waist that leaned close against the animal's body.

"Bat…trauks!" she yelled.

Chanse looked back and saw several on horses kicking up a cloud of dust in hot pursuit. And with them rode the large, dark figure of a man.

Four

THE NORTH FOREST

Her brother's grip squeezed the air out of her, as the animal beneath them cut a rift through the tall dry grasses as if its tail were on fire.

"Are they…still…behind us?" she shouted, her sentence broken apart by the horse's gallop.

"Dunno. Your…hairsin… myeyes!"

"I can't…s-seeither!" she hollered back. "The…horse's mane…keeps whipping me in th'face!"

The beast lowered its head, and she no longer felt the sting of horsehair against her cheeks. Chelly looked up. The edge of a forest rose like a dark wall just a few strides in front of them – and the horse showed no signs of slowing.

"Stop!" Chelly yelled.

The horse bolted into the shadows, unyielding.

"I…said…STOP!"

Dodging and weaving through a labyrinth of branches, the horse raced on. Its wide body scraping against trunks and limbs as the twins tried desperately to hang on.

"Pull back…on its mane," Chanse said.

"I'm…trying." She craned her head over her shoulder. "It…won't…listen."

As she turned back around, a thick mesh of branches knotted with her hair, jerking her off the animal. She collided with Chanse, knocking him to the ground, but her tangled tresses left her suspended several feet in the air.

"Chanse, help!" she cried, grabbing hold of the limb. She tried pulling herself up, but after several attempts could only hang by her arms to relieve her scalp.

Her brother lay on the ground, unresponsive.

"Chanse. Get up!"

His eyes flickered and blinked, dazed by the fall; his stare unfocused.

"Chanse."

He sat up and rubbed a hand across his face, wiping away the fog.

"Chanse, get me down!"

"Hmm?" He squinted at her.

"I'm stuck."

"Just let go. It's not that far."

"I can't. It's got me by my hair."

He jumped to his feet and shimmied up the tree.

"I'll cut you down," he said pulling a knife from his pouch and climbing out onto the limb.

"Hurry," she said, her arms already aching.

He grabbed a fistful of her hair.

"What are you doing?" she said.

"I'm going to cut you down."

"Not my hair! I thought you were going to cut the branch."

"Oh." Chanse let go. "Since when did your hair ever mean that much to you?" he mumbled, hacking away at the twigs.

Chelly's hands were cramping and her grip loosened.

"Chanse, I'm slipping!" Chelly cried.

"I'm going as fast as I can."

One twig after another cracked as he cut, but there were many more before she'd be free.

"Skip the twigs, just cut the whole branch!" she said as her left hand slipped off. "Chanse hurry!"

"It's just that this knife is kinda dull and rusty."

Chelly felt the flow of blood bring life back into her dangling fingers, and grabbed hold again with both arms. But her other arm screamed for release and lost its grip.

"I can't hold on any longer!" she said, grabbing again with both hands and straining to keep her fingers curled around the branch.

The whittling stopped, and she felt Chanse take hold of her hair again. Several quick slashes later, her hair tumbled down to her shoulders and she dropped to the ground.

"Sorry," Chanse said jumping out of the tree and helping her to her feet. "But look."

In the distance, she saw small black specks kicking up dust over the horizon.

"They're heading this way!" he said.

Chelly jumped up and darted into the forest with her brother. As they ran into the old-growth, the streams of setting sunlight that wove between the trees diminished until the dim blue light of shadow concealed them.

"We need to rest," Chanse said after getting a considerable distance from the forest's edge.

Panting, Chelly nodded. Her arms still ached and her lungs burned. She bent over and rested her hands on her knees.

"But this place won't do," he added.

She looked up at him, her brow furrowed. "Huh?" She couldn't believe he wanted to keep going.

"It's not a good place to hide."

"What do you mean? We could hide behind any tree."

"It feels too open and exposed. I wish there was a cave." Chanse took a few steps then glanced back. Chelly hadn't moved.

"Come on, let's go."

Taking her by the arm, Chanse pulled her along. They ran farther than she ever imagined she could until she thought her legs had turned to stone and only sheer determination picked them up and moved them.

The forest opened into a small clearing with three trees laden with ripe fruit. The only fruit they'd had in the mines was always mashed into brownish-grey sludge and indistinguishable by sight or taste. These, however, looked firm, plump, and beautiful.

Chelly picked one, collapsed under the tree, and bit into it.

"Hey wait!"

"What's the matter?" Chelly wiped the juice from her chin trying to keep the food in her mouth.

"It could be poisonous."

She chewed, exploring the texture and taste, then swallowed.

"Great. What if you get sick now?" Chanse looked angry.

She smiled, reached up, picked another, and tossed one into his hand.

"Only if you're allergic to pears."

"How do you know what they are?"

"Don't you remember? We each got one for our birthday when we turned five."

She could see by the quizzical look in his eye that she had jarred his memory.

"Really?" He examined the fruit in his hand.

She smiled and took another juicy bite. "You never did spend much time in the cooking room with Mom."

Chanse bit off a big mouthful and sat down.

Chelly picked another from the tree and sat next to him. For the first time since entering the mines, they satisfied their hunger, gorging themselves on the ripe fruit.

The sky had changed from blue to hues of oranges and reds, as clouds swam above silhouetted treetops.

Chelly looked up and wondered about their friends again. *Are they alive? Did they escape and find a way out, or had they been captured and forced to endure some unthinkable torture?* She kept her thoughts to herself, trying to believe the best like Chanse did, but something in her heart wouldn't let her. Every time she pictured their faces, she saw them disfigured in pain. And, always, she imagined Breena's eyes flooded with tears.

"Oh, I think I ate one too many." Chanse threw the half-eaten pear and stood up. "How about you?"

"I've been full for a while."

"We should probably take as many of these as we can carry. Who knows when we'll find food again." Chanse picked pairs from the lower branches and filled his pouch until its seams were about to pop.

"Why, where are we going?"

"I just don't feel safe without being in something. Anything can see us out here."

Chelly stood, ignoring her unwilling body, and pulled fruit off the trees. She didn't want to keep going but knew she couldn't dissuade her brother. So, when they had picked all they could carry, the twins ventured deeper into the forest.

* * * *

The horizon swallowed the last rays of sunlight when Dymorius found the branches strung with long locks of hair. *Interesting*, he thought, looking down at the ground and back up at the tree. Batrauks rode up next to him to hear his command.

"You, go find that horse and return it to the

stable by morning. It will not have gone much further. The rest of you follow me."

"Where?" A large grey was dumb enough to ask.

Dymorius grabbed the whip that hung from the pommel of his saddle, and with one flick cracked it against the grey's face. The Batrauk squealed and a large welt appeared.

"They are no longer on the animal, and we must rescue them of course," he said in a voice exuding calm and control as he recoiled the long leather braid.

He had spent much of the previous night at the feast and had risen early to break in new steeds. So, it had already been a long day when he returned with the newly tamed animals and spotted two young ones standing on his stable.

He couldn't believe his eyes when they dropped onto his finest stallion, spooking the beast into action and leaving him and his hoard on much slower animals.

*The fable of old...*He wondered. *Could it be true? Could it be happening?*

* * * *

The forest had turned to shadows, lit by a full moon shining through a misty sky. The air chilled and everything felt damp. Dew soaked through their clothes and Chelly shivered.

How much further does Chanse think we have to go?

The trees separated, opening into a small dell. A dead tree stood at its edge. The top had broken off and only a few naked branches remained.

"How about here?" Chelly said and sat on the ground, against the old tree. She leaned back and pulled her legs in for warmth.

Chanse walked around to the other side, reappearing a moment later.

"Hey, this tree is hollow. There's an opening in back down by the roots."

Too cold and tired, Chelly didn't respond.

"If we can get in, we'd be warmer than out in the open."

Chelly got up and looked. The hole appeared big enough to squeeze inside.

"What do you think, should we go in?" he asked.

"I don't know. Do bats live in trees?"

Breaking off a long branch he said, "There's one way to find out." He poked it into the tree, swishing it around and a small shadowy shape bolted out. Chanse flinched, jumping out of the way.

"It's fine," he said laughing at himself. "If a rabbit is safe in there, anything is. Go on in."

"You first," Chelly said.

"Fine. Just help me get some branches. I want to cover the hole after we're inside."

A thick layer of dry leaves covered the tree's cramped interior. Chanse reached back outside and covered the opening with the branches they'd gathered, then stretched out on his back and fell asleep.

Without enough space for them both to lie down, Chelly struggled to get comfortable, trying to sleep sitting up. If he's going to hog the whole place, I'll just use him as the bed. She thought and reclined across her brother, who didn't even stir.

After what seemed like only a moment, Chelly's eyes opened, awakened by the sound of horses and riders.

"You, go west. You two, head northeast around to the village near the bog and see if they've seen anything. Meet me here in the morning," a gravelly voice commanded.

"Ngraauk. Shouldn't we head back? You've been gone from the kingdom all day, and the night is half gone," a Batrauk said.

"And let those two little darlings stay out here, frightened and all alone? Besides, this is the most excitement I've had since hunting people in caves. Now get going, all of you!"

"Yes, Dymorius," they responded in unison.

Horses rode off in different directions, but someone dismounted near their tree opposite the opening.

It's him. Dymorius! Chelly's heart raced, pounding so hard she feared it would be heard. The sound of snapping branches was soon followed by steel against flint, then the crackle of a fire.

The flame's glow revealed a knothole in the tree. Chelly positioned herself to peek through the small window and saw their pursuer walking off into the woods. Chanse began to rustle, but Chelly put her hand over his mouth, waking him. She motioned him to stay still and silent.

"He's here!" Chelly whispered pointing at the knothole.

"He, who?"

"Dymorius," she said. "They were all here! When the Batrauks were leaving I heard them talking and that's him!"

Chelly heard a noise and held a finger up to her lips. Peeking through the knothole, she saw the figure return with more wood for the fire. Dymorius' silhouette rose in front of the flames as he walked over to the tree and reclined. Mere inches of wood and bark separated them from their pursuer.

Hours crept by and not Chelly, Chanse, nor Dymorius slept through the long night. As the air chilled, the mists rose and moistened the ground with cold dew. Black skies lightened to steel grey, as morning approached. And the branches Chanse had laid near the opening of the tree rustled.

The rabbit that had been flushed out of its home returned. Chelly looked through the hole at the fire. Dymorius was gone. As the rabbit crouched inside the entrance, she and Chanse reached out to grab it before it could give them away. Finding its home still occupied the animal avoided their grasp and scurried back through the opening. There was a high-pitched cry followed by a sickening crack then Dymorius' presence reappeared by the fire, a lifeless rabbit in his hands.

When morning broke, they heard the racket of Batrauks back from their search. Again, Chelly and Chanse positioned themselves behind the knothole.

"Didn't find a thing," Dymorius' small troop reported. A grey bent down, and picked up some small bones from the ground near the fire, and began gnawing on them.

"Ngraauuk!" he croaked and hopped with delight. "Good, wha-what was it?"

Dymorius slapped the bones from his hand.

"Rabbit!" he snarled. "Now let's get going. We've wasted too much time already. I've got to get word out to the borders about these two."

The fog had thickened. Dymorius and his Batrauks rode off, disappearing into the morning mist. The sound of their horses faded into silence.

"Let's get going," Chanse said.

The two crawled out of the tree and stood next to the embers of the fire a moment for warmth.

"Great, now where?" Chelly asked.

"Well, we're not going that way," Chanse said pointing in the direction Dymorius had gone. He took from his pouch the small metal object he had found in the cave. Tapping its edges against a stone, he pried at it. More rusted bits of metal flaked off as the lid finally broke open. Chelly gazed over his shoulder at the gadget.

"What is that thing?"

"It's a compass," Chanse explained. "One like Father had. I used to play with his."

"Oh, I remember. He always had it sitting on the small table next to his chair by the hearth."

Her brother looked lost in memory as he rubbed his thumb across its lid, and even in the morning's dull light, his eyes glistened.

"Does it still work?" she asked.

Chanse snapped out of his daze and thumped the compass with his finger. The needle swung freely. "It does," he smiled and pointed into the mist. "North."

"Why that way?" Chelly asked.

"Simple really," Chanse said. "It's not the direction we came from, and it's not where Dymorius, is heading…"

"You had to look at a compass to figure that?"

"And it's the direction of that other kingdom."

* * * *

Dymorius could feel his stature diminishing. He needed worship but knew what the old prophecy said and wouldn't sit by and let it come to fruition.

Something that had been agitating him all morning started to crystallize in his mind. *Why*, he thought, *did that rabbit run out of its hole? I should have had to fish it out – unless there was something already in there. Something to scare it. Something like...* "Those…!" he said aloud, jerking on the reins, and yanking his horse to a sudden stop.

His Batrauks halted behind him, their steeds prancing from the abrupt command.

"Come with me!" Dymorius commanded turning about and weaving his way through his troupe.

"My Lord?" a brown Batrauk said.

"We have more rabbits to catch," Dymorius grinned.

Back at the tree, he discovered branches had been removed from the hole where the rabbit had come out. A piece of fruit lay in the entrance and the telltale sign of footprints were pressed into the damp earth.

"They were here!" He threw the fruit against the tree and it splattered. "And you didn't find them." He pointed to the grey who had earlier inquired about the rabbit bones. "Where were you all night?"

"Out in the woods." The Batrauk shook.

"Doing what?"

The creature averted Dymorius' stare, his gaze darting back and forth between those of his kind. "Young ones," he twitched. "Loo-Looking for young ones."

"Well, why did you look for them out there when they were right here?"

"Told me to." The grey flinched, cowering.

"I am sick of your excuses! I distinctly ordered you to find those filthy little urchins, and you didn't!" Dymorius motioned to a brown Batrauk who rode up next to him.

"You and the rest, punish him. And make sure it lasts."

Dymorius mounted his horse and turned to watch the penalty. The faithful surrounded the accused, whose eyes bulged with fear as they piled on top and forced him to the ground. Beneath the scuffle came a muffled cry. A rope wrapped tight around his neck as the other end of it was flung over the highest branch of the old dead tree.

Dymorius felt power flowing in again at their obedience to kill, and it felt very good. He absorbed the moment like cancer absorbs life from a healthy body.

The rope pulled tight, cutting off the victim's last shriek. His feet left the ground. A single crow called, followed by the ruckus of a murder gathering for their feast, and Dymorius returned to his impressive size.

Five

HUNTED

Chanse climbed over a fallen tree from a forest much older than the one that grew around him now. These trees were smaller and flourished like weeds in the soggy soil, sprouting so close together that he and Chelly couldn't pass between them in places. And like anything small and numerous they were a nuisance, covering the ground with vine-like roots and hiding them with the yellowish-brown leaves they dropped.

"I'm tired. Can we sit down and rest?" Chelly asked, hoisting herself over the log.

Chanse looked around.

"Dymorius and the Batrauks are long gone the other way by now," Chelly added.

Chanse slumped down onto the soggy ground.

"Sure."

The day was cold and damp, and the fog had only worsened. In an odd way, he almost wished to be back in the mines where at least it was dry. Chelly opened her pouch. Pulling out two pieces of fruit, she handed one to her brother.

"Where do you think they are?" Chelly asked.

"Who, Dymorius and…"

"No! Breena, Drake, and Ricker."

Chanse swallowed the mouthful he'd bitten off. "Like I said before, they're probably halfway to that northern kingdom by now."

"Why do you think so?"

"Listen. There's no need to worry about them," Chanse snapped, digging his teeth into more pear.

"But what about Breena?" Chelly asked. "She wouldn't be able to keep up with those two."

"You know Drake wouldn't leave her behind. He may be too rough with her, but he protects her something fierce. So just…" Chanse stopped himself and his voice became gentle but firm like their father's. "Try not to worry. It doesn't help us, or them right now."

He swallowed his last bite, wiped his hands off on his dirty trousers, and leaned back against a tree. Folding his arms, he closed his eyes and listened. For the first time, he noticed how peaceful the forest sounded. The still air, the soft hum of insects, broken only by the occasional song of a bird off in the distance.

He could sense his sister still peering at him. "What are you looking at?" he mumbled, but Chelly didn't answer. Chanse opened an eye to peek over at her. She didn't glare at him as he had felt but stared off into the distance.

"Are you okay?" he asked.

Still no answer.

"What's wrong?"

She looked over at him. Her eyes glistened with tears.

"Nothing. I'm alright now," she said folding herself into her arms.

I'm supposed to believe that? Chanse tried to think of something to say, but he had no words of comfort for her. There were too many things he didn't know, couldn't know, so he closed his eyes again and ignored his sister.

* * * *

Dymorius sent three Batrauks east to travel the road that wound its way around the swamp to the village at the North end of the bog, while he and the remaining Batrauk went straight north, hoping the two were lost.

The undergrowth of the woods made it increasingly difficult to ride. He stopped and dismounted. Walking a few paces to relieve himself, he noticed broken branches and bent grass. In the soil at his feet appeared to be a footprint. Upon further examination, he found not one, but two sets of tracks heading north. A smile cracked across his face.

"The bog is not far ahead," he said adjusting his cloak. "Follow me. We walk from here."

He led the way stealthily through the thick tangle of trees with one faithful Batrauk stumbling along behind. Its large, flat feet flicked up leaves and got caught in the roots that lay across the rutted ground. The ruler thought it best to distance himself. Moving swift and silent, he went on ahead of his servant.

* * * *

A distant rustling broke the silence and Chanse opened his eyes. Chelly had fallen asleep across from him and he prodded her gently with his foot.

"Listen," Chanse whispered when she opened her eyes.

"What do you think it is?" Chelly yawned.

"Whatever it is, it's getting closer," he said. "We'd better get going."

They stood up and looked over the fallen tree. In the distance, a lone Batrauk stumbled in their direction, but looking down at his feet had yet to see them.

They each took a cautious step backward when the shadowy figure of their pursuer appeared from behind a much nearer clump of trees. Their eyes met and for a moment time froze. Chanse saw the expression on Dymorius change from surprise to glee.

Adrenalin flooded his veins, as he grabbed Chelly's arm and fled. All sounds ceased but that of his heart pounding in his ears. With Chelly beside him, neither the branches clawing at their skin nor the roots grabbing at their feet seemed to slow them.

The woods closed in ahead of them with trees growing too close together to pass through.

"We've got to turn around," Chanse said.

"Wait. Look." Chelly pointed to an opening between the trees and they raced through. On the other side the woods thinned and ahead lay an open field, flat and green.

Chanse ran full speed. As soon as he strode onto it, the ground gave way and he found himself sinking. He grabbed at the branches of a tree that hung above him and hoisted himself back to shore where Chelly had stopped.

"That's not a field," he panted, shocked by his discovery of a blanket of plants that grow on top of still waters. His clothes were drenched and heavy, covered with small leafy weeds. The watery overgrowth lay in every direction before them.

"We're trapped!" Chanse said, turning around and seeing their pursuer blocking off their only exit. Chanse and Chelly stood on the furthest point of the peninsula.

"I can't swim," Chelly said.

"Maybe we can wade across," Chanse said taking one step into the murky water. His leg sank through the weeds but could feel no ground. "Too deep," he said pulling himself back out.

"The bog is bottomless." Dymorius stopped and leaned comfortably against a tree. "Beneath the moss and weeds, there's nothing but water."

Chelly clutched Chanse's arm as they stood with their feet at the land's end.

"Better watch your step, you don't want to fall in," Dymorius said, slowly, snaking his way toward them. "Now tell me, what are two helpless little dears, like yourselves, doing way out here in the middle of the forest where you could get hurt?" His words came out smooth and inviting.

"We're going away, to another kingdom. A better one," Chelly insisted, holding tighter onto Chanse's arm.

"Oh, you poor disillusioned children. There is no other kingdom. You speak of something that doesn't even exist, it never has. It's a fairy tale."

"What do you mean it doesn't exist? We read about it in the diary we found in a cave," Chanse said, feeling the pinching grip of his sister.

"My dear boy, how trustworthy is that? I mean, you don't even know who wrote it," Dymorius said. "The author could have been a complete lunatic for all you know. I wouldn't trust my life – indeed my future, to something like that. Would you?"

Dymorius sat down on a boulder, blocking their only way of escape. He seemed calm and content and let his gaze wander about freely as if he were enjoying a picnic.

"You're lying!" Chanse said, his throat tightening around his vocal cords.

Dymorius glared up at him for an instant, revealing his charade, but caught himself and resumed his calm demeanor. Chanse glared back.

"What if he's telling the truth?" Chelly whispered.

Chanse's glower turned to shock. Dymorius smiled at him with a look of victory.

"Why would someone bother writing all that down if it wasn't true?" Chanse said between clenched teeth.

"People write things for their own amusements I suppose," Dymorius said still relaxing and picking at something between his teeth. "Or they think it fun to lead innocent people, like yourself, astray. But, if you really want to pursue someone else's distorted little tale, then I suppose you have that right. I do rule a free kingdom you know."

"Free?" Chanse's voice tightening again so that it squeaked. "Free to do what? Be taken away from our home? To dig ore and get beaten by Batrauks every waking hour? Free to not see the light of day or breathe fresh air? What free?"

"I can see that they've worked you too hard. I'll have to talk with those in charge of the mines and demand better care of my workers," Dymorius dropped his chin to his chest, his mouth downturned, and looked up at them. "It's my fault I suppose. I admit that I don't inspect the mines as frequently as I should." He drew a deep breath, "How old are you two?"

Chelly looked over at Chanse and just shrugged. They couldn't answer. Years beneath the ground without daytime or night left them without any idea of their ages.

"Why I'll bet you're close to twelve aren't you?" Dymorius stood and paced a bit, his head down, a hand rubbing the back of his neck as if in deep concentration. He snapped his fingers. "You two are probably coming up for a promotion. You'll be out of the mines soon and ruling over Batrauks yourselves. You know I could use the likes of you up in the higher offices. Honest, brave, and readers, that's unusual." He paced more. "And able to make decisions to change the conditions in those mines. Won't you help me to help your friends who are still back there? After all, it would be selfish of you to leave them there under those conditions, while you go around looking for this mythical kingdom."

"Help you to help them?" Chelly asked, confused by his proposition.

"Certainly!" Dymorius perked up as if he were a fisherman with a nibble on his hook. "You see, usually those promoted to watch over the young ones." Dymorius stopped and held up a hand as if to correct himself, "young adults really, they don't try to change anything for the better. When they leave, they only think of themselves. But you two have perspective. You're much smarter than they are, and readers, hmmm. You both hold much promise for the others."

Chanse could see the confusion on Chelly's face. He knew she worried about their friends. And if this meant a way to help them, she would want to try it. He had to break her concentration.

"If the other kingdom doesn't exist, then why are you trying so hard to keep us from going there? Why would you chase us all the way out here if there was no other place for us to go?"

Chelly looked crossways at her brother, the dreamy gaze broken. Dymorius' guard lowered and the expression on his face turned grim as he stopped in mid-step.

"I came out here to rescue two young ones,

who were in danger of getting lost in the woods, or coming to some terrible end. I found you two heading right into a bog, and you treat me like this? Where is your gratitude?" Dymorius' voice began to rise. "Dare you doubt my honor and integrity? I am your king!"

"You're a liar!" Chanse shouted as the two took half a step back, their heels hanging over the edge. "You came out here to hunt us down like you did everyone else who ever tried to escape your kingdom. For some reason, you either want or need us back as your slaves!"

An angry growl escaped Dymorius lips as he lunged toward them unable to control his rage. But Chanse grabbed Chelly and leaped backward into the bog where they disappeared beneath its dark waters.

* * * *

Chelly plunged through the weeds, and the frigid water took her breath away. She looked for Chanse, but couldn't see more than a couple of feet from her face before it vanished into an auburn haze.

Grabbing at the clumps of weeds that floated above her like little islands, she hoped to pull herself up for air. But with each try, she raised only a little before the hovering clod submerged.

Her lungs burning, her arms flailing for anything to get her to the surface, she felt a strong current pulling at her legs, tugging her deeper. The surface became an unreachable shrinking orb of light and she gave up. Her arms went limp, she let out the air she had been holding onto and looked down. Through the darkness appeared the open mouth of an enormous serpent already up to her waist surrounded her. It lunged forward to eat her – and with one gulp, it did.

* * * *

Dymorius stood, glaring at the waves being choked by the cover of weeds. Behind him, the Batrauk who had struggled his way through the forest arrived.

"Go in after them!" he commanded pointing at the bog.

The Batrauk looked at the water then back at his master.

"I said GO!"

The servant swallowed hard and stepped into the cold deep, his body floating easily near its surface.

"Go under and get them." Dymorius lost patience, picked up a stone, and hurled it at him. He missed.

The Batrauk sank beneath the weeds and algae only to resurface a moment later. The waters churned around him with a million ripples. The bubbling raced closer and closer. He turned back to shore, but before he could get there, it surrounded him. Dymorius watched in disgust and pleasure as a swarm of leeches consumed the Batrauk and drained its body of life, leaving it floating like an empty sack of skin.

Dymorius felt a surge of strength from the servant's fear, but he still hungered for worship. Though the leeches had gotten his Batrauk, he saw no similar sign of the twins' demise. Staring out over the bog he waited and watched as his soul gnawed at him for its craving. *Perhaps, if they survive,* he thought, *I could convince them that I sacrificed my Batrauk so that they would not be consumed by the leeches. That may bring them to their knees.* His appetite increased. But the water churned once more, only not with tiny ripples. This time, a large powerful wave broke the surface, and as the arched back of a serpent split the waters, he knew the pursuit had ended.

"Lousy creature!" he said kicking at a pile of leaves. Driven by his craving, Dymorius turned and left for the one place he wanted to be and the one thing he desired, a feast at his throne. Behind him, the weeds buffeted the waves and all became still.

Six

The Promise

Chelly felt the rhythmic squeeze of being swallowed as she slid down the creature's throat. A slimy secretion coated her, making her glide easily into its stomach. She let out a scream as something grabbed at her feet. Kicking at it, she could only imagine some internal tentacle ready to tear her limb from limb and make her easier to digest.

"Chelly, Chelly! Don't kick, it's me!" Her brother's voice startled her.

"Chanse, where are you?" She reached down, found his hand, and pulled herself to him.

"We can breathe," he said, and his hopeful tone offended her.

Chelly didn't speak. The fact that they were able to breathe could only be life's practical joke meant to prolong their suffering while mocking their meaningless existence. Their demise took hold, sinking as deeply into her as she had sunk inside the serpent. There was nothing more for them now but the pain of entering the eternal darkness of death.

"Chelly, I have two ideas," Chanse said

breaking the silence, but Chelly didn't want to listen. "I need your help deciding how to get out of here."

"Chanse, it's over," her voice trembled. "Look where we are. We're dead." She wiped the slime from her hand and felt the burning acid from the creature's stomach against her exposed skin. "You don't escape death, Chanse."

"I have two ideas," Chanse continued, ignoring his sister. "One is to move around with as much commotion as possible and maybe the creature will vomit us out. The other is for me to take my knife and start cutting our way through. What do you think?"

Chelly felt fear like never before. Not a panic type of fear, but that of complete despair. And she could not answer her brother.

"Well?" Chanse asked, grabbing her arm, prodding a response.

"Didn't you hear me? WE ARE DEAD!" She yanked free from his grasp and wanted to bury her face in her hands, but they were covered in slime.

"Don't forget who you are," Chanse said. "You are an Adaman!"

"So, what!" she yelled. "So, my last name is Adaman, is that supposed to impress this creature that swallowed us? Is it some magic word that can get us free? Because if it is, then why didn't we use it before in the mines?" As she spoke, slime dripped into her mouth. She gagged, spit it out, and cried.

"The morning we were taken, Dad took me aside and said, 'Chanse, guard your heart. They'll steal everything else from you, but they can only get your heart if you give it to them. And if you do, they'll kill it, then nothing will matter.'" Chanse spit out some slime that got into his mouth. "Don't give up Chelly! Life is always worth fighting for, even a terrible one!"

The sound of his words echoed their father's and pricked a hole in the darkness that encompassed Chelly. She thought of the book and slid her hand along her side feeling it in her pouch. She longed to see it and to hear her mother's voice again as she read it. Chelly felt the prodding and took hold of the thin strand of hope left there by her father and mother.

"If it vomits us out," she said after long consideration, "it may just swallow us again, and chew us this time. Not to mention how gross it is to be something's vomit."

"Good point. Now if I can just find that knife…"

"Just our luck, it's back at the tree with my hair."

"Nope. Found it!" Chanse said. "Well then – Here goes!" He put his back against her and thrust. The creature twisted in pain, gulping down water.

"Chanse stop!"

"No! It's working!"

He pushed hard against her. The monster twisted with more violence, and with each contortion swallowed more water.

"We're gonna drown," Chelly cried.

"Shove your legs up its throat! Don't let it swallow!"

Chelly maneuvered herself and, with screams of disgust, slid one of her legs up the creature's neck, then the other. The serpent shuddered and contorted; its reflexes trying hard to swallow its food.

* * * *

The pole rested in his relaxed grip as he stared out at the line. He remembered the stories of when this bog had been a huge, thriving lake, teeming with fish of all varieties. Those were the days of his grandfather's youth when the smokehouses were always full, tables were filled with fish, fried, smoked, or broiled and boats filled the bays.

But three generations had passed, depending on how one counted. So much had changed since they first spotted the monster. It came like a curse that took over their waters. The bays turned to weeds as what once had been fresh and clear turned acidic, depleting the population of fish as well as the population of people.

Sickness and plague swept through the land. The city turned into a town, then the town dwindled to a mere village, and they had changed their diet in order to survive. By the time he'd been born, fish had become a delicacy. He remembered eating them once when he was very young. He loved the way it flaked off the bone, and he could still taste the butter that clung to each morsel. That was before he was taken to the mines, and things had changed even more since then. He'd been back now for years, but fish were off the menu. Instead, the village made do with the ever-growing population of frogs and turtles. This became their staple, though he was not fond of it.

"Not a bite!" he complained to the other man in the boat.

"What did you expect? A fish hasn't been caught in these waters in a decade. You're a fool to keep trying."

"One day they'll come back, you'll see. 'When the waters churn and the…'"

"And the creature…blah, blah, blah," his fishing partner interrupted. "Just drop the old tales. I don't know why you even believe them."

"Larshal, you're a fisherman. You come from a long line of fishermen. It's in your blood. Don't you want to catch a fish?"

"Jarrett, get it through your head. Whether I want to catch fish or not isn't the issue!" Larshal snapped back. "There are no fish to catch. That's the only issue. Now drop that stupid pole and line and grab the net for frogs."

Jarrett would have kept the argument going if he hadn't seen a wave ripple in the distance. He pointed out at the waters that calmed as quickly as they stirred. "Did you see that?" he asked.

"See what?"

"We'd better pull in the gear."

The surface of the bog churned once more, as the creature burst up through the weeds and chunks of moss. They had never seen it act with such violence before. It thrashed about at everything in its path. The two men gathered the nets by the armload, disregarding any of their catch.

"Isn't it supposed to be dormant this time of year?" Jarrett grunted as he pulled.

"I guess it didn't check its calendar. Maybe you want to remind it," Larshal said when he gave a tug on the net that nearly sent him overboard. He tugged again. "It's stuck!"

The creature leaped out of the water, turned in their direction, and picked up speed.

"Forget the nets," Jarrett said taking the gathered portions from the bottom of the boat and tossing them over the side. "Let's go!"

In the distance, the beast submerged. They each grabbed an oar and sculled the vessel through the weeds and water.

"Thistle Bay is closest," Larshal said digging his oar deep into the bog. It hit something hard. "We need to hurry if…"

The boat exploded out of the water. Its bottom rammed by the creature with such force it catapulted them into the air. Looking down, Jarrett saw nothing but bog as he fell. But a strong tug on his cloak pulled him in and he landed in the bottom of the boat. As it rolled back righting itself, Jarrett braced his back against the seat, grabbed an oar, and kept rowing.

"Hurry, Hurry!" Larshal said as the monster turned again to pursue them.

Twisting along the surface, the serpent reared its large, ugly head into the air by its long, powerful neck. It fixed its eyes on Jarrett with its mouth agape, ready to devour.

Jarrett cranked back on the oar with all his strength, lost his footing, and tumbled backward. His oar dropped into the water.

The serpent hissed.

Between him and the monster, Larshal appeared screaming like a madman. He held his oar up like a spear ready to strike.

The creature's eyes rolled back in its head, its neck wrenched backward, and it splashed down beside the boat, drenching the two men and covering them in weeds. There it lay lifeless, floating on the broken chunks of bog.

Jarrett stared at the creature, wondering what happened. Why were they still alive? Larshal poked at it with his oar and the carcass bobbed up and down with the prodding. But it no longer stirred. Its massive body moved with the rhythm of the waves as they settled down to a ripple. Its eyes glared off into nothing.

"Come on!" Larshal said. "Let's drag this thing back and show everyone."

Jarrett knotted a rope and slung it around a protrusion on the creature's head as Larshal retrieved the oar that had dropped. Together they strained against the dead weight and towed it back to the village.

Once ashore, everyone came to see the magnificent kill. Jarrett gathered several men and they dragged the serpent on land.

"The beast that has terrified us for generations is dead!" Larshal said, and everyone gathered around him to listen. "It pursued us with the fury of a storm, attacking our boat as we fought to keep it from capsizing. I must say, we feared for our lives!"

Jarrett looked around at wide eyes and open mouths as Larshal paused.

"For only a moment. Then, gathering our wits and strength, we overcame it with nothing but our oars and our courage."

Jarrett felt Larshal's arm wrap around his shoulder and pull him in next to him. Larshal grinned at everyone as they all applauded, but Jarrett's smile lacked the same enthusiasm. He knew everyone would believe the tale, but he also knew the truth, and the truth wasn't as heroic.

While Larshal answered questions, Jarrett noticed something peculiar with the creature. Its belly lurched and moved. He stepped through the crowd nearing the corpse. Others turned and seeing the movement backed away letting out terrified gasps.

"No need to fear," Larshal said holding his arms up to draw back their attention. "The creature is quite dead. It's just reflexes."

Bending over the beast, Jarrett began to examine the oddity when a gash appeared and blood flowed onto the ground. He jumped back, gagging on the stench, as musty steam rose into the air. The wound parted and the gap became wider until out came a human hand, then a foot. More hands and feet emerged, and out of the creature crawled two youth covered in weeds, slime, and serpent's blood.

They staggered to their feet dazed,

speechless, and helpless, looking around at an audience of disgust and disbelief. Jarrett expected somebody to aid with warm blankets or something, but none came. Instead, women fainted, and men armed themselves as if these two were the creature's offspring. But, then the man Jarrett admired most stepped in front of them all. Dressed in his simple brown cloak, he lifted his trembling hands and addressed the villagers.

"Today, what was written to our forefathers is fulfilled!" He shook with excitement. "It is fulfilled before our very eyes!"

"What is, Elder?" some asked.

The man called Elder pointed to the two standing in the dirt, shivering, wet, and bloody. "Our forefathers were given a promise! We've read it from the scrolls and sang it in our songs!"

Elder was met with blank stares, but Jarrett hung on every word.

Elder gestured with his hands for everyone to stay where they were as he ran off. Moments later he came running back waving a scroll and shouting, "See, see!" He held it up before them all. "The prophet said that we would see deliverance from our bondage to the kingdom of Dymorius when this sign happened. Listen to what he told us."

Elder unrolled the scroll from its spool, his hands still trembling with excitement. He searched for a moment until his eyes landed on the passage he recalled. With a voice that seemed to cut through the confusion, he read:

'In that day the creature will stir,

the one you fear most will surrender to you.
And from its belly two will come,
a sign that your deliverance is at hand.'

"These are the two!" Elder approached and knelt in the dirt in front of them, his voice quivering. "Welcome to BorBoros, children of promise."

Seven

The Village

Steam rose from Chanse's body in the cool, damp air. He wrapped his arms around himself for warmth and felt the slimy fluids that covered him, ooze between his fingers.

A woman in the crowd moaned, bent over, and gagged. Others stood armed and unmoving, gawking at him and his sister.

The one who greeted them as the *Children of Promise* spoke to a dark-haired man, before running off into the village. The man he had spoken to stepped forward. Taking them by their arms, he said nothing but led them into the village away from the bog.

The people followed close behind as they approached a broad, round building. Short with small windows near its thatched roof, a constant column of smoke rose through its central chimney.

As they approached the door, the man let go of their arms and entered. Chanse trailed in tow, but before he or Chelly could step through, the door slammed in their faces. He turned to Chelly and then around to face the villagers.

"Chanse, what are we going to do? Are we in trouble?" Chelly whispered.

"What are *they* going to do?" he said under his breath, looking out at the crowd of stern faces.

A sudden rush of warm water hit them from above. They turned around in time to see the dark-haired man lifting another tub. Dousing them again, he rinsed away much of the slime and filth, then took them by the arm, rushed them into the warm building, and quickly shut the door.

Inside, a large fire pit stood in the center of the floor. Glowing coals had been shoveled beneath large brass tubs of water that lined its perimeter. Curtains hung from hooks that came out of the ceiling rafters that enclosed each bath.

"My name is Jarrett," the man with the dark hair said, "And this is the scrubhouse. You'll find changing rooms over there." He pointed to a row of small doors. "Where you can undress and then get into a bath." Then he left.

Chelly disappeared behind one of the doors, leaving Chanse by himself. He put his hand in the nearest tub and quickly pulled it out again. His skin tingled from the hot water. He put it back in and held it under. After a couple of seconds, he got used to the sensation, and much to his surprise, it felt inviting. Leaving his clothes in a pile at his feet, he hopped into a tub and yanked the curtain shut.

Sinking into the warm water, he examined his legs. They were scratched and raw, and the bath made them sting. He picked up a cake of soap from a dish that hung from the side of the tub and began to scrub, but the dirt on many areas refused to come off; it had somehow become part of its permanent color.

Hearing someone in the room, he called out, "Chelly?"

"Yeah?" she said.

He found it odd that her voice didn't come from where he had heard the noise a moment ago. A stream of grey light shined on his curtain then disappeared with the sound of a door latch.

Chanse peeked from behind the curtain. One other tub had its curtain drawn.

"Chelly, how'd we get here?"

"I think we died," she said. "This bath feels so good, we must be in paradise."

Chanse rubbed the bar of soap across his cuts and winced. "We're plenty alive," he said rinsing the suds off his wounds.

The warmth of the water relaxed his muscles, and he struggled to keep his eyes open. Again, the door opened, and someone called to them.

"When you are ready, clean clothes are hanging in the changing rooms for you. Let us know when you're done." Then the door closed. Chanse opened his curtain and looked out.

"I suppose that's our cue to finish up," he said.

"You first. I'm too comfortable to even move right now." Chelly yawned. "I didn't know it could feel so good to be clean!"

Looking around Chanse saw Chelly's towel by her tub. "Hey, where'd you get the towel?" he asked.

"Hanging inside the little door," she said. "I grabbed it when I got undressed."

He looked and two doors were left open, each with clean clothes laid out on benches, and one with a towel hanging from its peg. Hopping out of the tub, Chanse dashed toward the one with the towel. His wet feet glided easily on the smooth stone floor and he slipped backwards toward the tub. Reaching out to get his balance, he grabbed hold of the curtain. But one by one the rings let loose and he fell flat on his back with the curtain landing on top of him.

As he untangled himself, Chanse saw his sister peeking at him and laughing. He crawled over to the changing room, keeping the curtain around his waist, and went in. A moment later, he opened the door just enough to throw out the curtain.

Later he emerged fully dressed and embarrassed. "I'll go let them know you're almost done," he said.

"Watch your step." Chelly laughed.

"Very funny," he mumbled and walked out of the building.

* * * *

Chelly got out of the tub, although she didn't want to. She toweled off in the closet and put on the clean clothes they provided. On her way out she passed a mirror made of polished bronze that stood against a wall. Walking over, she looked into it. She saw her uneven crop of hair and wondered what it might have looked like had it not been cut in such haste by her brother. As she stared, a woman came in and stood beside her. Pulling up a chair, she motioned for Chelly to sit. She did, and the woman picked up a brush and scissors that sat on a nearby table and proceeded to work at her uneven mess.

She watched the transformation in the polished bronze reflection. Her hair, now clean and neat, touched upon her shoulders. Overwhelmed by the act of kindness, Chelly couldn't speak. Her sincere thank you came out only as tears.

The woman who stood behind Chelly caught her gaze in the mirror. She rested her hands on Chelly's shoulders, then smiled and nodded.

"My little girl is just about your age now," she sighed before her voice cracked. "Her name is Tara. She is in Tartrus."

Chelly knew many faces in the mines, but there were hundreds, if not thousands of the young and not many became friends with names. Chelly looked at the woman in the reflection and felt that she should say or do something.

As if reading her mind, the woman smiled. "You've done so much for me already." She stroked Chelly's hair once more with the brush and her smile quivered away. "You've given me hope." The woman set the scissors and brush back on the stand, turned, and hurried out of the scrubhouse.

* * * *

Chelly entered the largest building in the

village, which bustled with commotion. Tables of many shapes and sizes covered its floor and were filled to capacity. The air was heavy with the smells of food.

Chanse had already been seated at a table and was drinking a steaming brew when others escorted Chelly in. They sat her next to him on a platform and brought her a cup like the one he had. In it steamed the same dark liquid. She brought it up to her face smelling the bittersweet aroma. Blowing on it, she pressed the cup to her lips and drew in a sip. Her face scrunched up.

"It's not as sweet as it smells." Chanse laughed.

Chelly put the cup down and looked around. Others seemed to be enjoying the drink. So, she tried another sip. With a grimace, she placed it on the table and resisted the urge to push it away.

"How can you drink this?" she asked her brother.

"I can't. I just hold the cup to keep my hands warm. Now and then I lift it to my face and take a whiff. I like the smell." He brought the mug to his nose, closed his eyes, and inhaled the bittersweet aroma. When he lowered it, he looked up at her. "You fixed your hair."

"One of the ladies came into the scrubhouse after you left and undid the mess you made."

"Yeah, sorry about that."

Chelly pulled it away from her face, tucking it behind her ear. "She asked if I knew her daughter back in the mines. She said her name is Tara." Her chin dropped to her chest and her hair fell forward.

"Do you?"

Chelly shook her head. "I wish I did. If you could have seen her face, the way she looked at me. She wanted her daughter."

"Look around you. Everyone has or knows someone down there. They all feel the same way."

"Then it's how Mom and Dad must feel." Chelly gazed into the steam rising from her cup. "Chanse, I want to go home."

Chanse put his arm around his sister's shoulder and pulled her in. The noise and bustle faded away and she rested her head on his shoulder.

He sipped the strange brew. "Nope. Still not good."

The man in the brown cloak who had sounded so excited by their arrival walked up to the platform and instructed everyone to sit in their places. The room grew silent as people bowed their heads. His eyes closed, his voice solemn, he started thanking someone, but Chanse looked around and couldn't tell who he addressed. He didn't speak long, and when he finished all the people said the same word at the same time, one he had never heard before. It must've been some kind of signal because as soon as they said it, they all helped themselves to the dishes of food on the tables.

Chanse took the cue and filled his plate by the spoonful, as Chelly looking quizzically at the menu.

An old gentleman sitting next to them leaned forward. "That is wild rice mixed with cranberries," he muttered pointing to the large dish in the center of the table. "And these," he added holding up a clump of greasy, finger-length morsels, "are fried frog legs." He then chuckled to himself and put one in his mouth. A moment later he pulled it back out cleaned to the bone.

Chanse inspected them closer and held one to his nose. With a shrug, he bit into one. Smiling, he shoveled a big scoop of them onto his plate next to what could have passed as a hill of wild rice with cranberries.

More than pleased with the taste of the rice and berries, Chelly ignored the frog legs and finished more than a plateful.

As the meal ended, the man in the brown cloak stood up on the platform. Again, he addressed the people and re-emphasized the words he had spoken when they arrived.

"These are them of whom it is written," he said pointing in their direction.

Some cheered and others shook their heads in disbelief before he continued to explain.

Chelly couldn't focus. And the harder she tried, the fuzzier things became. She blinked and someone else stood where the man in the brown cloak had been a second ago. Her head dropped forward and she twitched back to consciousness. Chelly pinched herself, squinted her eyes at the speaker intent on staying alert, then everything faded away.

Eight

The Meeting

Chanse woke up in a small room and a warm bed. Across from him, Chelly lay sound asleep, wrapped up like a cocoon in a layer of blankets. The morning sun streamed through panes of glass covered with sheer yellow curtains, filling the place with a golden light. He had no recollection of how he got there from the evening meal. Maybe the bath, the warm drink, or the full belly had brought on the deep sleep. He pulled the covers up under his chin and rolled onto his side trying to recall what had happened.

"Good morning."

Chanse sat up with a jolt and shook his head, startled that he had fallen back asleep. The man in the brown cloak stood beside him and held out a bowl.

"Although, I must say the morning is all but gone," he laughed.

"Good morning." Chanse reached out to accept the steaming meal.

"Careful. I reheated it so it's still quite

warm."

Swinging his legs out from under the covers and over the side of the bed, Chanse noticed all except his undergarments had been removed and he wore some sort of long shirt that reached down past his knees. He wrapped the blanket around his shoulders warding off the chill in the air and set the bowl on his lap.

The breakfast consisted of steamed rice mixed with raisins and sugar. He lifted a spoonful to his mouth.

"You're the one who keeps talking about us aren't you," Chanse said as he shoveled in a bite.

"My name is John. I am called the Elder in this village."

Chelly stirred in her bed. Rolling over, she blinked several times.

"I thought this was all a dream." She smiled and propped herself up on her elbows.

"And good morning to you, miss," Elder said.

"Thank you," she said as he handed breakfast to her. But the smile left her face as her fearful gaze darted back and forth searching the room.

"What are you looking for?" Chanse mumbled, his mouth full of breakfast.

"My pouch! Where's my pouch?" she cried.

"Your things are hanging near the door," Elder pointed. "We tried to clean your clothes but there wasn't much we could do about them. So, we have new ones for you. They are folded at the foot of the beds," he said pointing.

Chelly put her dish on the floor, hopped out

from under her covers, and grabbed her pouch off a peg where it hung.

"It's too light!" she said. Her hands undid the drawstring and she reached inside.

Elder sat down on a stool. "You must be looking for this," he said holding a small book out to her. She snatched it from his hand and stepped back.

"What's that?" Chanse asked.

She hugged it tight to her chest. "It's mine. Mother gave it to me the day they took us away," she said.

"Yeah, but what is it?"

"It's a book," Elder said. "A very dangerous book. That's why, when I came across it, I took steps to make sure no one else found out about it." He rested his elbows on his knees and leaned forward. "I've never seen an actual copy before. They were banished a long time ago. All known copies were seized and burned. I can't imagine how this one survived."

"What's so dangerous about a book?" Chanse shot a glare over at Chelly. "And why haven't you shown it to me before?"

Elder sat back and rubbed his hands across his knees. "It's only dangerous because of the times we live in. It's actually very special. You see it was written by the rightful king. Some say the path of every person's destiny can be found hidden within its pages. That's why Dymorius hates it so much, and why all known copies were destroyed. I believe he wants to take away our purpose, our individuality… he wants to turn us into a mob with the single purpose of worshipping him."

"How'd you get it?" Chanse dropped the spoon into his empty bowl with a clang.

"Mother gave it as a kind of birthday present," her voice trailed. "That's why I never showed you. I didn't see you with anything and didn't want you to feel bad. Besides, she told me to keep it hidden."

"But how were you able to keep it with you when we were sent into the mines?" Chanse asked. "We weren't allowed to take anything in with us."

"When we were being searched, I thought for sure it would be found and I'd lose it. But just as I neared the beginning of the line, the girl in front of me started screaming. She was so frantic and the Batrauks were so distracted, that I just walked past. So, they never really searched me. The book brings me luck."

"I believe it's something more than luck. This book is powerful. That's why I stayed up all night reading it from cover to cover," John the Elder admitted.

"The rightful king," Chelly repeated. "It's true then, there is another kingdom."

"Aren't we already out of Gehenna," Chanse asked scooting back on the bed and leaning his back against the wall.

Elder laughed. "No, I'm sorry. You are both still in the kingdom of Dymorius. Though he doesn't exercise quite as much authority here, since we're so far removed from Tartrus. He rules over us through a delegate of his, a man by the name of Unwyn, who can also be vile. Fortunately, he left two days ago for Tartrus. He was called in for a meeting after Batrauks came here looking for two runaways. He should be back by week's end, so we don't have much time. I can't imagine the trouble there will be if Unwyn finds you two here. But to answer your question, yes, there is another kingdom, over the mountains."

"Is it good?" Chelly asked.

"Why don't the people here leave and go there?" Chanse added.

"Unwyn keeps a heavy hand on us, and the borders are heavily protected in the months when the mountains are passable. Even then, no one is sure of the way to get through them." Elder looked down at his hands as he spoke, then lifted his gaze. "And yes, we believe it is a good place."

He stood up to leave and placed his hand on the latch of the door. "I'll come back to escort you to the meeting house after you have eaten and dressed. We are all interested to hear your story." He smiled. "Then we will decide how best to help you." The door opened and he stepped across the threshold but turned to them. His eyebrows knit together. "One more thing." he paused and lifted a finger to his lips. "Only I know about the book so you're best to keep it secret … for your own safety."

He left and the door clicked, latching behind him.

"Why are they so eager to help us?" Chelly asked when the sound of Elder's footsteps faded away.

"I'm not sure." Chanse picked up the pants

that lay folded at the foot of his bed and put them on. "Except that, for some reason…" He pulled off the nightshirt. "They think we can help them with something." The brisk air hurried him along, and he pulled the new shirt over his head. "Anyway, we're going to leave here as soon as possible and make our way home."

The word "home" slipped out of his mouth before he could catch it. Chelly looked at him with a stare of confusion.

"I want to go home too," she said.

Chanse didn't respond. He slipped into the stockings and shoes. They were well worn but fit. "So, what's it like? – The book, I mean."

Chelly sat motionless on the edge of the bed just staring at it. "I've only read a few parts," she said, her voice quiet. She took a deep breath. "I guess I don't know, it just seems like some stories of people who did brave things, some poems, some strange sayings. I don't really understand it."

"Do you think you could read some of it to me sometime?" Chanse asked fumbling with the leather straps that fastened the shoes. "Chelly?"

"Hmm? Yeah, sure," she mumbled coming out of her daze. "Once we're out of Gehenna I'll read the whole thing to you."

"You'd better get moving," Chanse pointed at her bowl of nearly untouched breakfast.

"I guess my appetite isn't awake yet." She took a few bites then got dressed. They left the room together. John the Elder sat outside under a tree waiting for them.

"That was quick," he said rolling up a small scroll, the same one he had read to the villagers the day before.

"Mr. John the Elder?" Chelly said.

"Most just call me Elder," he chuckled as they walked the well-worn path through the village.

"You seem to understand something of this book that I don't. Can you teach it to me?"

Elder stopped and looked around. Then, pulling them close, he whispered. "Your book is very special indeed. I wish I knew more about it myself. You must realize, your book is more than just a story; it is THE story. The one about all of us, who we are, why we are, even what we are," he said pointing at his heart then put his hands on their shoulders. "I would love to read it with you two – someday when it's safe."

Chelly lit up at Elder's offer. Something Chanse hadn't seen since before they were taken from their home. Her bright smile and the twinkle in her eye that looked like their mother's, took him by surprise, and he wasn't sure why but he felt jealous. He was still surprised at her secret and it left him a little miffed, especially now that it seemed so important.

They continued along the wide dirt path into the clearing of the village square. The doors of every building were shut and windows darkened; it appeared abandoned. No signs of anyone outside or in. Elder led them to a large round building with a thatched roof. There didn't appear to be any windows, but two large wooden doors carved with ornate scenes of mountains and a great city hung on iron hinges. Elder stopped in front of them.

"Wait," he said. "Stay right here. I need to go back and grab my other parchments. I'll be right back." He hurried off down one of the many paths that led away from the lodge, like threads of a web converging at its center.

"What was that all about with you getting so excited back there?" Chanse asked.

"I just want to learn more about this book," Chelly said. "Before I just read it because I could hear Mother's voice when I did. I felt close to her. But now I want to actually understand it."

Elder came running back down the path. "Well, let's go in," he said opening the door for them.

A great noise exploded out of the building. The whole village seemed to be inside deliberating over a topic of great debate in not-so-friendly terms. But when they saw the twins, all fell silent. The doors swung shut and Elder led them to a riser at the center of the room. Light shined down through a small, multi-paned window in the center of the roof that lit the twins from above with intense light. The first row of people encircling them was a mixture of expressions. Behind them, the rest sank into shadow.

Chanse felt the stares of a hundred strangers piercing him. He got the impression that they were on trial and sank deep into the chair he'd been offered, hoping this would soon be over, whatever *this* was.

Elder walked up and stood at the end of the platform. "As I mentioned to you outside, my name is John, but most just call me Elder, because I teach the old beliefs of our fathers in this village. Please introduce yourselves to us."

"My name is Chanse and this is my sister, Chelly. We're twins." Chanse fidgeted in his seat.

"Chanse, Chelly, we are honored to have you here. The people of BorBoros have all gathered here to listen to your tale, and we're all excited to hear it. You see – we believe you have a great deal to do with our future."

How could we have anything to do with their future? Chanse thought. *We don't even know these people.* He passed a quizzical look to his sister, who shrugged in return. It didn't seem to him that she realized the weight of what John the Elder just said. She just smiled and listened.

"So, tell us, how did you come here from the serpent's belly?"

Chelly began to relay the story as Chanse watched the expression on Elder's face. It started out serious and quizzical, but as the tale moved further along, his eyes widened in astonishment. Chanse heard gasps come from the shadowy mass along the walls when Chelly spoke of the horse and the night in the tree. And the level rose as she told of being trapped at the bog.

"I thought we were doomed," she said, "when Chanse grabbed me and threw us both into the water."

Chanse took his eyes off Elder and looked over at the smirk of blame on her face.

"How was I to know a monster lived in it?"

Chanse said. When the laughter of the crowd subsided, he added, “Besides, it turned out alright.”

Chelly rolled her eyes. “Anyway, that’s how we ended up in its stomach. It swallowed us.”

“That is incredible! Simply incredible,” Elder gasped.

“Incredible indeed,” said a tall silhouetted figure standing near the now open doorway.

Chanse didn’t like the tone of voice.

“I believe it’s more like trouble.” The figure made his way toward John the Elder and stepped into the light. He stood a head taller than Elder, with broad shoulders and dirty blonde hair that hung past them.

“Larshal, we’ve got nothing to fear,” Elder said, “Unwyn will be gone for at least two more days.”

“There will be trouble when he returns,” Larshal said. He stepped onto the platform looking down on the twins. The light above him shadowed his deep-set eyes, but Chanse could sense his stern expression. “He’ll find out they’ve been here and have to tell Dymorius, who will then bring punishment on us all.” Turning toward the crowd he continued, “I say we turn them in ourselves and avoid this mess.”

The people murmured in their seats and the atmosphere in the room changed to dread. Whispers escalated into a loud hum until Elder spoke up.

“Friends, friends, don’t you realize what has happened here? The bog creature that has terrorized us for over a century is dead, and prophecies are being fulfilled! This is a sign of our deliverance from Dymorius! We will again be free men! We can't hand over our only hope to our enemy. The prophecies must go on to fulfillment!"

"I am not a man driven by fear or superstition." Larshal interrupted. "I fought the monster. I killed it with my own courage and brought it here. You can keep your prophecies, Elder. I'm not going to invite the armies of Dymorius into our village now that our real enemy lies dead on our shore!"

People rallied behind the one named Larshal and cheered him on. Elder tried again to speak but they were beginning to uproar. A large man grabbed Chanse and Chelly, lifting them out of the chairs. His arms were like small tree trunks both in size and strength, and his grip pinched tight around Chanse's arm shooting pain down to his fingers.

"Where should we put them?"

Larshal took charge. "In the lockhouse, until we can make provisions to take them back to Tartrus."

"You can't do this!" Elder said, stepping toe to toe with Larshal.

Larshal turned away. "Put Elder in there too, so he can't cause any more trouble."

The mob moved on Larshal's orders, pulling Elder and the twins out of the meetinghouse. They dragged them to a stone building on the other side of the village and threw them in. Elder fell to the floor from the shove. The door slammed shut behind them and the lock clicked.

Chanse wondered what had just happened. It seemed to him that one minute the village was ready to help them in any way possible, and the next they were criminals. He ran over to the door and struggled with the handle to see if it would budge. When it didn't, a knot formed in his gut.

"They're making a big mistake," Elder said, picking himself up off the floor. "This is the time of the fulfillment. This is the beginning of our deliverance! Why don't they see?" His hands were clenched into fists as he stared at the ceiling. Turning to the twins, he apologized. "I'm sorry. Really, very sorry for the way they're treating you. I never would have thought they'd behave like this. Please forgive them and forgive me."

Chanse looked over at Elder, whose head hung in shame, his brow furrowed and eyes welling with tears. It was the face of someone whose hopes had been raised to incredible heights, only to be dashed. Chanse knew the feeling. He had felt it the day of his sixth birthday, the anticipated celebration, the gifts, and the iced cakes. He couldn't understand why his parents had ignored it or suppressed it whenever he would remind them of its coming.

Chanse remembered the elation he felt waking that morning. He bolted out of bed and ran into his parent's room exclaiming, "It's our birthday!"

To his surprise, his mother and father were already up and his mother was crying. That's when his dad took him aside for the talk.

Chanse looked over at Elder. "I'm sorry we

brought you trouble."

Elder lifted his gaze to them. "You amaze me. How can you think of anyone but yourselves at a time like this?"

"No." Chelly looked at him and then around the room. "Nothing is amazing about two runaways being locked up in a cell."

Nine

A Guide

The lock clicked and the door opened. Jarrett, the man who had brought the twins to the scrubhouse the day before, stepped in with a tray of food.

"Bless you Elder," he greeted, bowing his head and setting the tray on an old barrel in the corner. He shook Elder's hand leaving in it a scrap of torn paper, then stepped back through the door. It latched shut.

Elder looked down at the crumpled wad in his hand and opened it. The corners of his mouth curled up as he read.

"What is it?" Chelly asked.

The worried look from his eyes faded, and a smile lightened his face.

"Come here," Elder whispered, drawing them in close. "You know that kingdom you asked about? Well, that's where you're headed for tonight." He lifted the tray of food off the barrel and opened its lid. "Jarrett, you…" Elder's voice rose with excitement. "He must've known something like this would happen. He is a faithful believer." Inside the barrel, the tray was set on were two packs, each stocked with provisions for the journey.

"There's one missing!" Chelly said looking up at Elder.

"I won't be going with you. I may still be able to talk sense into the people once they see you've gone. Anyway, while I'm here doing that, you'll be gaining a better head start than if I accompanied you."

"But we don't know the way," Chanse said.

"Jarrett will be your guide. He's a good man and knows the old roads. He has been as far as the foothills of Asher. From there you will cross the mountains. On the other side, is the kingdom you're looking for. But we must wait until the cover of night, which won't be for several hours. So, for now … rest."

A tall candle sitting on a shelf lit the room. They sat in silence, eating the meal that had been delivered. Chanse wolfed his down, but Chelly had a hard time swallowing. She hated the fact that their fate now lay in the hands of people they didn't even know. She reached into her pouch and pulled out the book for words of comfort. Then holding it out to Elder said, "Please?"

Elder's hand trembled as he reached for it. Clearing his throat, he opened it to the first page and read.

Chelly listened, amazed at the things she hadn't seen in the book before. Elder would read a passage, then pause, as if to soak in each sentence and verse before relaying its meaning. He even took notes, picking up a light-colored stone and marking up the floor with quotes he wished to remember.

Into the night, he unfolded secrets that lay hidden in its stories, and Chelly listened spellbound. She felt energized unlike ever before as each tale made life itself somehow clear. She had never felt this when reading it in the mines. In fact, like everyone else down there, she often questioned why she existed at all. Life seemed at best to be pointless, or worse a cruel joke.

As the hours passed, the candle melted down to a nub, with dripped wax hanging off the edge of the shelf. A rapid tapping at the door signaled that the time had come. Elder thrust the book back into Chelly's hands and he helped her up. Strangely, she wished they had had more time in their cell.

"Be brave," Elder said, ushering them to the door without hesitation. It opened and the twins were swept out into a moonless night, leaving John the Elder in the lockhouse to face the villagers in the morning.

Outside, Jarrett led them around the corner of the building. He pulled out two hooded cloaks from under his own and handed them out.

"Here, put these on," he said, looking over his shoulder. Chanse and Chelly fumbled with them in the dark.

"Here, like this," he said adjusting them. "We must move quickly. Follow me."

Jarrett led them through the village. At first, buildings looked like large black holes dotting the woods under the starry sky, but the twin's sight adjusted easily to the darkness. They often saw things in the dark before Jarrett bumped into them.

For the rest of the night, they fled through the forest without uttering a word. When morning came and the edge of the sky turned golden, Jarrett stopped. Ahead of them stood a series of old stone walls, the remains of a large building. Chelly marveled at the size of the stones that reached to such a height.

"Go ahead and rest you two, we've got a long way to go and you've been clipping along at a good pace," Jarrett said, then laughed. "I forgot that you see so well at night. I did too when I first came out of the mines. It'll wear off though in time."

"What was this place?" Chelly asked captivated.

Broken archways and the remains of massive pillars were overtaken by the dense forest, leaving the place looking mysterious and enchanting.

"Our great grandfather's city. This building was their meeting hall," he said leaning against one of the pillars. "It was glorious, especially compared to the mere hut we use now."

He reached into his pack and pulled out a leather pouch, held shut by a drawstring. Opening it, he took out some dried frog meat and offered it to the twins.

"How far are we from the mountains?" Chanse asked taking a bite.

Chelly nibbled on the morsel he handed her, imagining that it must have tasted better when it was warm and crispy. It stuck in her throat and she swallowed hard several times just to get the first bite down. Hiding the rest behind her back, she dropped it to the ground.

"We're a three-day journey from the mountains. We could see them from here if we could get above the trees. This meeting hall used to tower above them, and our forefathers enjoyed the view of the mountains from its many balconies." Jarrett pointed at the remains of doorways high up in the stone walls. "I wish I could have seen them," he said as if dreaming.

"Those were days of freedom when we were known as Asherites. That was before Dymorius rose to power and destroyed our city, banishing us to live on the bog."

"It must have been spectacular," Chelly said looking up and envisioning it towering above the treetops.

"Yes," Jarrett sighed, "it must have. But I've only heard the stories like everyone else. Every year we read them at the meeting house to remind us of the day when we move back here and rebuild it."

"When will that be?" Chanse asked.

"Not as long as Dymorius rules, I'm afraid. But that's not the only problem." Jarrett took out another piece of dried meat, pulled the drawstring shut on the pouch, and slipped it back into his pack.

"What do you mean?" Chelly asked.

"Well, most have lost sight of the promise and don't believe it will ever happen. They think prophecies are merely stories to encourage us and are not to be taken literally. Just look at the way they turned on Elder – and you."

"I thought he'd be more respected than that," Chelly said.

"Maybe in my father's day, but not now. Every generation that Dymorius rules, hearts grow colder. They lose sight of a future; they lose hope."

"Every generation?" Chanse asked, his mouth full of frog meat. He swallowed. "How old is Dymorius?"

"Some say he's immortal."

"So, he could rule forever then?" Chanse took his last bite, wiped his mouth with the back of his hand, and rubbed it on his leg.

"Maybe. But another prophecy tells us that our city will be rebuilt. And that can't happen as long as he's in charge."

"Then when will it happen?" Chelly asked.

"No one knows for sure. Some prophecies allude to his rule lasting to the third or fourth generation, so I'm hoping to see it fulfilled in my lifetime. I'd love to be one to set my hands to rebuilding our city." He shouldered his pack. "Come. We must keep going if we're going to get the two of you over the mountains of Asher. Winter comes early there. If it has already begun, we will not be able to cross at all."

"Why are you helping us?" Chelly asked.

"The prophecies tell of two who will come from the serpent as a sign of our deliverance. You can guess how many times that has happened." He pulled his pack tight against his back and started walking.

"None, I suppose," Chanse said hurrying to catch up.

"Actually, two other times. Once, before I was born, a couple of men thought they'd kill the creature. They lured it in with poisoned fish and snared it with ropes."

"What happened?" Chelly asked trying to stay in step with Jarrett and Chanse.

"Just when they thought they had it secured, the creature rolled violently. The men were tangled in the ropes and yanked into the depths of the bog and – well, eaten."

"I know the feeling," Chanse said.

"Yes, I suppose you do." Jarrett laughed. "The poisoned fish must not have set too well with the creature, because days later, it vomited their bodies back onshore."

Jarrett pulled on the straps of his pack and hoisted it higher up on his back.

"But the other prophecy says they must escape the rule of Dymorius. Some insisted that, since those men no longer 'lived' in Gehenna, it was fulfilled and they began looking for Dymorius' reign to come to an end."

"That didn't happen," Chanse said.

"No, it didn't." Jarrett shook his head and picked up the pace.

"What about the other time?" Chelly asked.

"Hmm?"

"You said something like this happened twice before," Chelly said. "What was the other one?"

"Years ago, before I was sent to Tartrus, five unfortunate souls went out to check for cranberries too early in the season and were attacked by the creature. Three of them were devoured, and two managed to escape. The people of BorBoros were so worked up about it, that some claimed it was 'as if' they had come from the serpent, and again many began looking for Dymorius' reign to end.

"A lot of people stopped believing in the faith of our fathers after that. This time it's different though."

"How?" Chanse asked.

"You two came out of the creature, which is now dead. And it's the third generation under Dymorius. The only part left is to see you over the border, and we'll be free again as Asherites, not the people of BorBoros."

"How can we be as important as all that? You're talking about cities being rebuilt, people being set free, and kingdoms coming to an end, all while looking at Chelly and me." Chanse shook his head.

"Are you certain that only two escape?" Chelly asked.

"Yes. The writings specifically say two." Jarrett stopped and the other two halted. "I need to tell you something you may not know. I was in the boat with Larshal that day we brought in the creature. It charged after us and we both thought we were going to die. But then it collapsed – right in front of our boat. Dead! And do you know what I felt?"

"Um, happy?" Chelly guessed.

"Relieved?" Chanse asked.

"I felt a surge of excitement like never before, like something great was going to come of this. And when you two crawled out of its belly I was dumbstruck. I had listened to the prophecy and took it seriously, but never imagined it quite so literally. I guess my faith has faltered as much as anyone's."

"But Larshal said he killed the serpent with his oar," Chelly said.

"And courage," Chanse added with sarcasm.

"Yes. Well, Larshal tells tales like a true fisherman I suppose, but we had nothing to do with that creature's death. We only hauled it into shore. The real heroes, the ones who killed the creature ..." Jarrett pointed at them and walked off leaving Chelly and Chanse staring at each other.

"Are you two coming?" he hollered back.

Their journey continued until the sun dropped behind the trees in a gradient of rich cool hues. The twins were exhausted, and coming to a grove of white-barked trees, they lay down in the long grasses beneath.

"The season is changing early," Jarrett said looking up at the leaves. "The leaves have already turned gold. Go ahead and sleep." Jarrett sat up against a tree. "I'll keep watch."

Chanse drifted off quickly, but Chelly wondered what had become their friends and of John the Elder.

* * * *

The first rays of light sifted through the trees, illuminating the small village of BorBoros. As the door of the lockhouse opened, Larshal's silhouette filled the doorframe, his broad shoulders burdened with packs for a journey to return the twins. He looked around confused for a moment, stepped in, and grabbed Elder by the cloak.

"Fool! Where are they? What have you done with them?"

"Your freedom lies in their hands Larshal. You don't really want to throw it away."

Larshal slammed him against the wall. "Dead men aren't free, only dead!"

They stared at each other until Larshal eased his grip and let go. He walked to the door, looked out at the village, and drew a heavy breath. "And that's what we'll all be now, thanks to you."

He left and the door locked behind him.

John the Elder trembled as he slunk back down onto the floor. He wondered how far Jarrett had gotten with Chelly and Chanse, and how much time they had before Larshal led a band of others to go after them.

The bell rang from the village square.

Larshal must be calling a meeting. No doubt a search party will be rallied and ready to go within the hour. If there was only some way to stall them.

He had hoped that half the day would have gone by before they would come for them in the lockhouse, rather than starting this early.

Hanging his head onto his chest, Elder saw

the words he had scratched onto the floor from Chelly's book. And then he did something he had never done before – he called out to its Writer. It felt like the natural thing to do; yet foolish at the same time. Did he really think the Writer could read his mind or perceive his thoughts? Several times he thought about stopping these imaginings of help coming from a power capable of influencing far-off situations, but for some reason he believed against hope that he was heard, somehow.

No sooner had he let out the desires of his heart, than the lock turned, and they summoned him to an assembly. Unkempt from a sleepless night and his altercation with Larshal, he stepped into the darkened room of the meetinghouse, escorted by the force of three men. A single chair sat in the light of the platform, and they forced him down into it. Larshal stepped out of the shadows and addressed the people.

"Because of John the Elder here, we're going to have a visit from Dymorius and his army. When he finds out we've helped the two young ones escape, our end will be certain! Dymorius is ruthless. If we stay here, he'll come to our door. If we run, he'll hunt us down. Either way, we're all as good as dead!"

The screams and shouts of the villagers raised into a wall of protest. They yelled insults at Elder, while the sides of Larshal's mouth turned upwards. With the village frightened, Larshal could win their support and get them to do whatever he wanted. Elder decided that it didn't matter. One thing had to be done – drag the meeting on as long as possible and give Jarrett as much time as he could to get those two out of Gehenna.

The prophecy must go on to fulfillment, he reminded himself.

"Our only hope," Larshal said, stepping onto the platform next to Elder. He lifted his arms and the crowd quieted. "Our only hope is to keep him in the lockhouse until Dymorius arrives and hand him over. Since he's the one who let the two escape, maybe Dymorius will be satisfied to take only his life, and we'll be spared. But we must also make an effort to find them. Jarrett and I..."

"Wait!" Elder interrupted. "Don't I have a right to defend my actions? Or do you think I merely wanted to bring destruction to my friends, my family, and myself at the hands of a tyrant?"

"A prisoner has no rights," Larshal said through gritted teeth.

"We have heard what the accuser has to say in these matters. I believe it is in our best interest to also give an equal hearing to the defense." A gentleman dressed in a wool coat with brass buttons stood in the open doorway. Tall and straight he stepped forward. Elder knew the voice well, its authoritative timbre made him hard to ignore even for his adversaries. He entered the room, which fell silent.

"Wilyam, it is a pleasant honor to see you among us again after so many months. I hope all has been well with you," Elder said.

"As with you, John. Can you please explain what has happened to turn our fine people into this rabble?"

Larshal's face twisted with frustration. Wilyam was a direct descendant of Asher, firstborn of his clan, and last of their true delegates. Elder could see that with Wilyam back, Larshal's plan to retrieve the two prisoners would move at a much slower pace. And for Larshal, reason had a pesky way of looking at too many angles before making a decision.

"The most amazing thing! The day before yesterday," Elder began retelling the story of how the creature had died, and how a boy and girl emerged from its belly. Wilyam listened with wonder and awe at what he heard as Elder addressed the gathering.

"You all heard me mention the fulfillment of prophecy, as the two named Chanse and Chelly, came out of the serpent's belly. Many of you know by heart the other prophesies as well that pertain to this event, and what it means for us and our freedom. But, let me remind you of them again and explain their meaning."

He took the scroll that he kept with him and unrolling it. Finding the passage, he read the prophetic messages, which spoke of an end to the reign of Dymorius and the rebuilding of their city.

"Interpretations of fairy tales are not going to defend you against the armies of Dymorius!" Larshal shouted, pacing and raking his fingers through his hair.

"Was the creature that you brought in, a fairy tale, Larshal? Were the two who climbed out of its belly, as was foretold to us, a mere fairy tale? Or did these things happen? Yes, they happened! We know they did. They happened for our benefit and encouragement so that we might stand against the fear and wickedness that has enslaved us for generations!" Elder said.

"I don't put my life in the hands of any prophecy when I can see our fate clearly. We still have a chance to find those two, and hand them over to Dymorius – if we'll act now! Look at the time we've lost already listening to your ramblings. We've wasted almost half of the day. We must act now! Jarrett and I will go find them and bring them back, dead or alive! Then you'll see who the real heroes are."

"But Larshal, where is Jarrett?" Elder asked.

For a moment every eye looked about the room for Larshal's missing partner.

"Jarrett is your friend, he's always there to help you. Yet he saw the truth and acted on it, in hope that he would be one of the first to help rebuild our city and its grand hall of meeting."

Larshal squinted, his eyes cold and hard. He grabbed the packs he had filled for the journey of returning the twins and stormed out of the meetinghouse.

Wilyam turned and addressed the village. "Neighbors, friends, and family, we are in a difficult situation, and this will be a time of great challenge and change. Therefore, we must consider carefully our plan of action."

Wilyam continued speaking of the village's great history and the city that was once their rightful place. He reminded them of the former things when they were the people of Asher, and that their fate need not lie in the mud of BorBoros if they would only take hold of their courage and stand for what they believe.

When he had finished, the people dispersed, hopeful and yet afraid.

"You've done our village a great service, John, but our job has just begun. These people need to be prepared for an inevitable battle to come," Wilyam said.

Elder shook his head in dismay at the threat of war. "I understand," he said, "and I wish it didn't have to be."

"But it must; we both know this to be true."

Elder did not respond, his heart filled with a mixture of excitement for their future freedom and dread for the people who would have to give their lives to secure it. *Maybe not*, he wished.

Wilyam's firm hand landed on Elder's shoulder. "Freedom is never voluntarily given by the oppressor. Come, John, let us discuss our possibilities."

Ten

Followed

Storming out of the meeting, Larshal ran across the village to the only road leading into it. The old forest highway, which had deteriorated into a vague path from generations of neglect, branched off less than a mile away, and he was sure Jarrett would have taken it.

Coming to the crossing, he saw a familiar figure rounding the bend, Unwyn had returned from Tartrus. Larshal, who never had personal dealings with the man, approached him.

"Unwyn!" he said and stepped toward the barrel-chested man. The man's lip snarling as he made his way to the other side of the road to pass by. Larshal knew Unwyn did not like mingling with the people of the village. In fact, he did not like the village of BorBoros at all anymore. Even though he craved his seat of power, he preferred his stays in Tartrus, meeting with other delegates, gorging himself with finer foods, and being intoxicated at Dymorius' worship festivals. As he walked past, Larshal cleared his throat.

“The two Dymorius is looking for have been found.”

The man stopped in midstride. His eyes became fixed on Larshal. “Where?”

At first, Larshal met the gaze, as man to man. But as the story progressed, Unwyn’s stare intensified like an alpha dog asserting dominion over the pack and Larshal found himself looking away. When he reached the part about the escape, Unwyn exploded in anger.

“How could you all be so stupid!” he yelled, lifting the walking stick he held in his hand. Everyone had seen him swing it in his fits of rage. Several unfortunate victims who didn’t move swift enough had met with the worn brass knob that decorated its handle never to forget it.

Larshal flinched. “I know sir.” He then explained his plan to go after Jarrett and the twins and turn the escapees in. Unwyn lowered his stick.

“I will go immediately back to Lord Dymorius,” he said. “And inform him that the village found the escapees and locked them up, but because of John the Elder, they have gotten away and that now the whole village is going after…”

“But I’m the only one going after them,” Larshal interrupted.

“I know that,” Unwyn glared at Larshal, his eyes cold and piercing. “But what do you think our Lord would rather hear, that everyone is after them or that just one man bothered to do so? Which is going to keep his wrath furthest from BorBoros and me? Would you rather have me disposed of and

Batrauks overrun this pathetic village?"

"You're right." Larshal nodded.

"I will also inform him of the direction they are going in case you fail to retrieve them in a timely manner. Now go! Get them back dead or alive or there will be Gehenna to pay." Unwyn turned to leave. "Wait!" He turned back again. "What do you have in those packs?"

"Provisions for retrieving the prisoners."

"I have a full day of travel ahead of me thanks to your people. Give me food to carry."

He opened a pack and let Unwyn take what he wanted, then parted.

Larshal followed the Old Forest Highway, entering the city ruins by nightfall. Resting among the stones, he built a small fire. It illuminated the ancient columns and archways reminding him of the songs that told of rebuilding.

Foolish dreams, he told himself.

He crossed his arms and reclined against the wall when a white spot on the ground caught his eye. He reached over and picked it up. *Frog meat.* Larshal grinned. He put out the fire and grabbing the packs ran off to continue the pursuit.

* * * *

"Wake up you two." Jarrett held out two steaming cups. "Take some tea."

Chanse sat up, accepted a cup, and nudged his sister.

Chelly rolled over and took the drink in both hands. Holding it up to her face she breathed in the vapors.

"Here are some dried berries and pine nuts to eat." The twins set the tea down and Jarrett poured the contents of a pouch into their hands.

"I'm amazed at how dry these cloaks kept us, considering the ground is soaked in dew."

"Living on a bog, we've learned how to make material that is warm as well as resistant to moisture."

"What's it made of?" Chelly asked.

"You don't want to know, but I will tell you it is a long process."

Chelly snuggled into her soft, warm hood. "You've got to tell me."

Jarrett smiled. "Well if you must know…"

She brushed her cheeks against the fabric.

"We weave them out of spider's legs."

She threw back her hood and shook out her hair.

Jarrett laughed. "Come on. We must be off." He stood up and walked away leaving two packs for the twins to carry.

Chanse threw a pack over his shoulder, grinning.

"What's so funny?" Chelly asked.

He nodded in Jarrett's direction. "Woven spider's legs."

"You think he's just kidding?" she asked examining the fiber of the garment.

"I think he's waiting for us to catch up. Let's

go."

Chelly grabbed her pack and they raced to meet up with Jarrett.

Clouds gathered in the morning light, their wispy bottoms glowing with brilliant hues of pinks and orange. It dazzled the twins, who couldn't stop gazing up at them.

"I remember my first year out of the mines," Jarrett said. "You probably don't even remember skies like this, do you?"

They shook their heads.

"Well, take one last good look, because the more you gawk at it, the slower we go. And I need you to get moving."

By mid-morning, the sky turned a flat grey that made their traveling both dreary and hard.

"How far do we hope to get today?" Chanse asked.

"The edge of the forest by nightfall and tomorrow the foothills," Jarrett said.

By mid-day, it began to rain and the three travelers took shelter under a canopy of trees, which were turning a deep purplish-red. Among the tallest in this country, Jarrett told them that they were among the last to turn their colors in the fall. It would not be long before winter made its way down the mountains and covered the land with snow.

"The rain is a blessing today," Jarrett said as they rested under the protection of the trees eating their midday meal. "They're bound to be after us by now, and it will wash away our trail, making it harder for them to follow us."

"Do they know where we're going?" Chelly asked him.

"Yes, they do. Though I've taken us along the northern ridge, which should save us time even though the terrain is harder. Still, they do know where we're headed. That's why we need to keep moving." Jarrett took another mouthful, and after swallowing asked, "How are the two of you doing so far?"

"I just like being outside, but Chelly's starting to limp a little."

"I'm fine," she said and looked at him crossways.

"Then let's get going," Jarrett said. He put the food away, tied the packs, and pulled up his hood.

The sound of their feet trampling the wet ground offset the rain's unrelenting tapping. As they climbed the northern ridge, a valley swept off to their left, and the terrain became rocky and uneven. Ahead, cliffs jutted out of the hillside. The incline grew, leaving them winded as they marched on. Nearing an outcropping, Jarrett stopped, waiting for the twins to catch up.

"Doing all right?" he asked.

"I need a rest," Chelly said leaning against the wall.

"Okay, a short one then." He put his tin cup down beneath a large leaf that acted like a funnel catching the rain. "But remember, for every rest we take, they get that much closer to us." He lifted the cup and took a swig.

"Alright," she said, her face blank of any

expression, jaw dropped, mouth open, and chest heaving.

Chanse tilted his head back with an open mouth and swallowed the rain.

"Chelly, how many times did we beg for a drink in the mines?" he asked.

"Plenty," she said panting.

After the short rest, Jarrett urged them to push on. "If we continue," he said, "we'll be at the edge of the forest before the night is halfway through."

"We're not as far as you expected then?" Chanse asked.

"Not quite, but the hardest trek of the day is over," Jarrett said.

"I don't think I can make it any farther." Chelly leaned against a tree and crumpled to the ground. Jarrett offered to carry her pack if she would keep going, and she agreed to let him. But it lasted only half an hour before she dragged behind.

"How are we doing?" Jarrett asked.

Chelly just shook her head.

"It's been a long day," Chanse said, seeing his sister's struggle. "And I need to stop for the night."

Jarrett closed his eyes, drew in a deep breath, and released it. "Alright," he said. "I think there's shelter just ahead. Not far, I promise."

A bitter chill came with the onset of a dark, starless night. They followed the cliffs that rose out of the hills like ominous towers and found a few small indentations that offered little protection from the rain and wind. Jarrett passed them by, while the twins voiced their disappointment.

"There are some caves around here that'll offer real shelter if I remember correctly," he said and continued on until they came across one that went deep into the hillside.

"Stay here," he said. Going in, he lit a candle from his pack and left the twins in the entrance. Several minutes later he returned.

"In the far end is a large, dry sandy spot where it will be comfortable to sleep."

They followed him deep into the cave, past large boulders and around bends, to where they found an area large enough for all of them to lie down. In the candlelight, the twins dug some food out of their packs. When they finished eating, Jarrett put out his candle and they sat in the darkness too exhausted to sleep.

"Is that a song?" Chanse asked, hearing a melody being hummed.

"Of course," Jarrett responded.

"What is it?"

"An old one the village sometimes sings when gathered to hear John the Elder speak. It tells of the promise of rebuilding the ancient city."

"Will you sing it for us?" Chelly asked.

"I don't remember any songs," Chanse said.

Jarrett cleared his throat. "I'm no singer, but I will try - for as long as you can bear it."

Though days are dark with sorrow
And night seems long and pale
And freedom lies before you

Slain with arrows

The curse is not forever
Though four lifetimes may assail
For Asher flows inside you
Through your marrow

The City will be great again with walls to guard around it
And gates of silver hang upon the hinge
But never locked, for fear will be
A long-forgotten memory...

He paused, hearing the deep breathing that meant the twins were asleep and finished the last line of the song to himself.

When freedom comes to Asherites again.

Inside the cave, the elements were held at bay, no rain to drench them, no wind to steal their warmth. Jarrett felt sure that he had come across the perfect haven to spend the night. Rolling onto his side, he let himself drift off into a deep and dreamless sleep, unaware of the dark figure that entered the mouth of the cave.

Eleven

TRAPPED

Chanse sat up, his sight adjusting quickly to the darkness. Unsure why he woke, a distant noise turned his head toward the entrance of the cave. *Jarrett must be up looking for something*, he thought and went to see if he could help.

Rounding the corner, a small flicker of candlelight caught his eye. He stepped forward before realizing it wasn't Jarrett. Larshal's broad shoulders were turned away, and Chanse dropped behind the wall and into the shadows.

He listened. The noise of rustling, mingled with incoherent mumbles, stayed at the cave's entrance. Chanse dared to look.

Larshal rummaged through his packs as he settled down for the night. A large knife fell to the ground. Larshal picked it up. The glint of the candle reflected off its blade, sending a small beacon into the dark. He gripped the handle in his fist and ran his finger down its edge before sheathing it into his belt.

Chanse couldn't hear Larshal's thoughts but could see the wild look in his eyes – the look of fear mixed with anger. The way Dymorius looked right before lunging at Chelly and him, making them jump into the bog. Only now there was no place to jump; they were trapped.

His heart drummed so loudly in his ears that Chanse thought it would echo off the cave walls and give him away. He closed his eyes and relied on the only thing he knew to calm himself. He imagined becoming nothing, sinking into obscurity like a stone on the cave floor. Inconspicuous. Unnoticeable. Nothing. The panic subsided. His breathing slowed. He disappeared.

Strong hands laid hold of him, one upon his shoulder and the other over his mouth. If his legs could have moved, they would have catapulted him through the ceiling of rock and earth, but they were pinned. Eyes opened wide, Chanse expected to see Larshal. It was Jarrett instead. He lowered his hand from Chanse's mouth, then motioned him to follow. Silently, they crawled back deeper into the cavern.

"I'll keep watch," he whispered.

"What are we going to do? We're trapped."

"No. He doesn't know we're here, and he's not going to."

"If he finds us, he'll kill us. I've seen the look in his eyes, he's crazy."

"He is my friend. Now just try to sleep, we've got a long night ahead."

Chanse sat still with his back against the wall, and though he remained silent, he couldn't quiet his mind. He was certain he would remain awake until morning, but the dark deceived him, for he couldn't tell if his eyes were open or shut, and in fact, he had drifted off into a dream that mirrored their predicament.

* * * *

Chelly stirred from her slumber, feeling aches in her legs from the long trek of the day before. She rolled over and opened her eyes. Light filtered into the place where she and her brother lay in shadow. Jarrett had gone, and she sat up to let the fog of sleep leave her head before grabbing her pack. Her feet hurt as she stood, and she couldn't help but think of what agony it would be to walk on them all day again.

She found Jarrett sitting with his back against the wall toward the entrance of the cave. His eyes were closed and he looked asleep but spoke to her as she approached.

"They have caught up to us."

He explained what had happened in the night and that he had kept watch, seeing Larshal leave right before the sun came up.

"What are we going to do?" she asked.

"We are going to let him get a couple hours ahead of us. Then we can follow him at a safe distance."

"But won't we have to pass him to go over the mountains?"

"Yes, but we'll just have to figure that part out when we get there." Jarrett turned to go back into the depth of the cave.

"Wait! Where are you going?"

"I've been keeping watch all night. If I travel on with the little sleep I got, I won't last past midday. So, if you wouldn't mind keeping watch, I'll grab a few more winks. If Chanse wakes up before I do, tell him our plan."

Chelly nodded and Jarrett disappeared to the back of the cave. A few short minutes later, his snoring echoed to the entrance.

It's a good thing he didn't fall asleep on watch, she thought, *or we would have been caught for sure.*

Chelly stretched and digging through her pack found something for breakfast. She took it, along with her book to the entrance of the cave where she could read by the light of day. Taking a mouthful of nuts and dried fruits, she set her things down, took a moment, and stepped outside. To her left, she saw the course they had traveled, just as steep as she had thought. Before her, the earth sloped away into valleys and hills cluttered with trees and ponds. To the right, Larshal's tracks led away in the cold wet soil, climbing higher still. The cool, crisp morning shown bright under a clear blue sky. An easy day for hunters to spot their prey. The sound of her fingernails clicking together caught her attention, and she shook her hands to stop it.

He's already gone past us. There's no need to worry about him anymore, she told herself to calm down.

Fresh air greeted her in gusts that wrestled the trees pulling off their leaves. She watched them dance their way to the ground until the chill forced her back into the cave's entrance. Chelly took another mouthful of breakfast and sat down in a spot where the sun streamed in and warmed her. Pulling out her book, she began to read. Now that John the Elder had explained some of its meaning, the stories seemed to take on a life of their own, and she felt that life filling her.

All grew quiet. Jarrett's snoring stopped and even the wind drew back from making the trees shudder. Chelly read in the stillness until a particular part of the story puzzled her. She read it again, put her finger between the pages, and closed the book. Looking away, she pondering its meaning. The sun now filled the entrance of the cave with light that gleamed off something lying among the stones. She squinted and got up to see what it was.

That's strange. I don't remember Jarrett having...

The sound of heavy steps outside stopped her as she reached out to pick up the blade. Her heart raced, she froze and listened intently. They drew nearer. With shaking hands and weak knees, she grabbed her things and ducked back into the darkness.

Peeking out from behind a boulder, she noticed the prints she left behind in the dirt and dust. And the more she looked, the more they stood out. Chelly swallowed hard; she had to do something.

Maybe if I hurry I can brush them away. The thought was fleeting but strong.

She hesitated, and in stomped Larshal. He

grumbled his frustrations to himself, as his frantic shuffling erased her footprints. He looked around, and seeing his blade, picked it up and ran out; trying to regain the ground he thought he'd lost.

Chelly relaxed, letting out a long exhale. She hadn't realized that during the entire time he was there, she had been holding her breath. Her hands, too, had been clenched so tight that they were red and sweaty. She decided that it would be safer to wait in back with Chanse and Jarrett and crawled back to where they slept.

Surrounded by silent darkness, Chelly wrestled with the words she had read from her book. They alluded to predetermined events and things that had been foreordained. But if they were destined to cross the mountains, why should it be so difficult? Wouldn't everything, every power, every decision, every action, and reaction pave the way for them to accomplish what the universe decided would happen? But what if she died? Would that just prove that she and Chanse were not the ones to fulfill the prophesy, that everyone's interpretation had been wrong? Or what if she quit? Could she influence the plan of ages by her small, weak will?

The restless stirrings of her brother interrupted her train of thought as she pondered all these things. Chanse tossed and turned, then sat up and hustled outside. Chelly grabbed a pack and followed, but stopped when she heard the spraying of water outside. He returned wiping his hands on his cloak. She winced.

"Let me see that pack, I'm hungry."

"Gross!"

"What?"

"You aren't putting your hands in here after… after getting them all wet."

Chanse laughed. "They were wet because I ran them through some wet grass to clean them off."

She handed him the pack reluctantly and he rummaged through it, as she told him what had happened while he'd been asleep.

"How long ago was that?" he asked.

"I don't know, about an hour."

"Let Jarrett sleep a while longer. The more distance between us and Larshal the better."

Chelly agreed. She sat down in the sunlight near the entrance and pulled out her book again. Chanse sat next to her.

"Would you read some of it to me?" he asked.

"Isn't it wonderful?" she smiled.

"I guess so."

Chelly looked at him, puzzled. How could he not be spellbound by these stories the way she, or Elder, or anyone else were for that matter?

Chanse just sat with his back against the wall, eating breakfast of nuts and berries and waiting for her to read.

Chelly began where she had left off. And every once in a while, would look up at her brother searching for signs, an expression or a light in his eye that would signal to her that he saw it, that he felt its draw. But she only saw in his face distraction.

The reading continued until Jarrett appeared from the back of the cave. His disheveled form stumbled out of the dark, rubbing his eyes and drawing his hand down his now stubbly chin.

"We've got to get going."

"But Larshal is only about an hour ahead of us," Chelly said, proceeding to tell him what happened.

Jarrett stepped out and looked at the sky, the cold breeze blowing his hair back. "The wind has changed direction. I fear winter is coming early. I'm afraid that if we don't get you across in the next few days, there will be no crossing."

He stepped back into the cave and in mere moments reappeared with all their gear. "We'll have to deal with Larshal, if or when we meet up with him," he said. Then, handing them their packs and shoveling a fistful of food into his mouth, they left.

Temperatures dropped as the day went by, but the cloaks they had been given kept them warm. Jarrett said he was leading the way up a steeper route than he originally planned, trying to avoid running into Larshal without losing time. Climbing higher, trees became smaller and scarcer. No longer were the trees a canopy above them. They could see the mountains of Asher ahead, rising like a great barrier, an immense wall to keep in prisoners. They paused when they came to the top of the high ridge they had ascended, and Jarrett looked for signs of Larshal.

"Maybe he gave up and went back," Chanse said.

"No possibility of that, I'm afraid. He's far too stubborn. But he isn't our biggest problem in crossing."

"What do you mean?" Chelly asked.

"Dymorius has these borders guarded heavily by Batrauks until winter when the mountains are impossible to cross. If they are still there, Larshal may inform them of our coming. If that is the case, they'll be watching. If they are not there, then winter has already come to the mountains and we are too late to make it over."

"What would we do then?" Chelly asked.

"I'm not sure," Jarrett said bending a long blade of grass in his hands and scanning the horizon. "Maybe try and hide you back in the village until spring, but that would be very difficult with Dymorius still looking for you."

Chelly started walking. Chanse took the cue and they picked up their pace.

"Hey, wait for me," Jarrett said running to catch up.

They didn't stop for lunch, instead, they ate more dried goods as they traveled, including that frog meat that Chelly didn't like. This time, however, hunger dictated more than taste and she ate all she was given. By late afternoon they had left the woods behind. In front of them, the landscape gave way to rolling foothills that lay barren and treeless, the tall grasses became coarse, and the golden hues of harvest faded into a dull grey. Beneath them, the earth was dry and uneven. Small, thorny bushes with gnarled branches that tangled together in clusters, dotted the crevasses between the hills, making it difficult to pass through the ravines they had to traverse. The hills offered them little protection from the wind, which increased and brought with it a bank of colorless clouds that hung just above the mountains.

As evening came, Jarrett found a sandy embankment, along a dried-up riverbed, sheltered from the now wintry gale. The three of them, weary and wind-beaten, pulled food out of their packs. It all seemed tasteless, and even after eating, Chelly's stomach gnawed for something satisfying. She remembered the wild rice and cranberries she had feasted on their first night in BorBoros. *That would be wonderful*, she thought and closed her eyes for a moment, envisioning a plate heaping with it.

Feeling a poke in her side, she opened her eyes and saw Jarrett holding something out to her. Annoyed by the distraction she took and examined it.

Handing a chunk to Chanse, he urged them to eat it.

The dark brown food wasn't like any meat, or plant, or fruit she'd ever seen before. Chelly held it up to her nose, it smelled sweet, then touched it to her tongue before deciding to bite into it. A small piece broke off and rested on her tongue until it softened into a creamy pool in her mouth. She swallowed. It filled her mouth with sweetness as she'd never known before. She took another bite and sucked on it, savoring every moment. Looking over at her brother with a smile, she raised her eyebrows with approval.

Chanse had already popped his whole piece into his mouth and chewed it up. He swallowed it before realizing the taste. When he did, his eyes widened with surprise. He looked at his sister who still had much of her portion left and wondered aloud if Jarrett had brought more.

Jarrett smiled.

"I thought you might like it. It's rare and I was fortunate to get as much as I did. You see, it used to be fairly common in our city. People ate it almost whenever they wanted. But when Dymorius took over, the plant that it's made from started dying off, and now there are only a few left. You've just eaten about half of what I brought, and I'm saving the rest to celebrate with when you get over the mountains."

The twins agreed that it would be the perfect treat for such an occasion.

Jarrett went straight to work, pulling out a tarp from his pack and laying it on the side of the bank. He held down its top and two sides with heavy rocks. With light fading fast, they all crawled beneath the tarp from the opening in the bottom side. Folding it under his feet, Jarrett showed the twins how to keep the wind from gusting up underneath. They all reclined into the sandy bank, digging out comfortable niches that gradually contoured with their bodies. As night drew on, the wind swept through the embankment, finding them at every worst possible moment. It wrestled with the tarp, taking its corners and shaking it violently, always waking them just as they were about to fall asleep.

* * * *

Larshal paused. The outpost that housed the

Batrauks stood before him and still there had been no sign of Jarrett or the twins. He contemplated turning back and searching for them via another route? But then if he missed them again and the Batrauks found them instead he would have failed, leaving the village in great peril.

Larshal didn't like his options. He still feared the Batrauks from his own days in Tartrus, even though he was stronger now. The memories of those creatures left him weak and vulnerable. He had worked very near the tunnels that were used as torture chambers and had seen too many go in and not come back out. But things were different now, he reminded himself, he was older and not confined to the darkness. Larshal looked down at his hands – they shook as he approached the outpost.

From a distance, he could hear the commotion of doors swinging open and slamming shut as each Batrauk went about his duties. Drawing closer he could see the creatures stacking what looked to be piles of provisions beside the main hut.

Larshal ignored the rhythm of his feet bringing him ever nearer, and instead focused on the wind stinging his face. He wondered how they were able to withstand the cold with their thin skin. He thought again of turning back until one Batrauk noticed him and alarmed the others. One by one they dropped what they were doing and came forward armed with clubs to confront him.

"Wait," Larshal said as they circled him. "I am on assignment by Dymorius to bring back two children, a boy, and a girl, who are trying to escape."

"We've no such word," said the one in charge, a brown with the first scars of a leader upon his shoulder. He ordered the others to apprehend him.

"No! You're making a mistake." Larshal raised his arms with open hands as a sign of surrender.

"We'll see," said the brown. "Our dispatch orders come in the morning. We will get news of any such thing then. But for now, you can spend the night in the shed."

A sharp blow to the back of the head and all went black. When Larshal came to, they were shoving him into a small building. The door slammed shut and locked before he could get up. Frost covered the walls of the small room, and from the penetrating cold, he realized he'd been stripped of his cloak and packs.

He pounded against the door, cursing the Batrauks and insisting that they release him.

"You moronic toads!" he shouted, "When Dymorius hears of this, your legs will be cut off and fried…do you hear me?"

When most men would have become silent, Larshal yelled out his demands for release. A hatch in the door flew open, and a bucket of icy water drenched him.

"That ought to cool you down!" One voice rose among the laughter.

The tiny door slammed shut and Larshal sat down in a corner tired, frustrated, and angry. Although his rage burned, he shivered. The metal floor and walls shuddered in the wind, making them colder than the ice that formed on his clothes and face. He curled his legs up and wrapped himself in his arms, but it was impossible to get warm. For the first time since the search began, he realized that he was exhausted. Now wet, cold, and hungry, it wasn't long before he quivered uncontrollably and wondered if he'd survive the night.

Twelve

Abandoned

A breeze swept across the meadow, churning the grasses like a sea and ruffling the pages of an open book. The one holding it ran his hand down the center of its spine, making it stay open. The warm morning sun shone brightly across the hills and onto the reader who sat against the trunk of a great maple that had turned fiery shades of red and orange. He looked up as a figure clad in armor of burnished bronze rode up on horseback and dismounted.

"Your Majesty." The warrior bowed before him.

The king placed a marker between the pages and closed the book. "Are you prepared for battle?"

"Yes, your Majesty! Always."

"Very well. Assemble a full regiment and be ready to leave with me at dawn tomorrow. It will be a two-day ride to the border. Bring extra provisions, we hope to be escorting others back with us."

"Yes, your Majesty."

The warrior held his bowed position.

"Is there a question?" the king asked.

"Your Majesty, if I may, who might be coming?"

"The promise is being fulfilled and those who were chosen are on their way. They will need our assistance, as I'm sure Dymorius will not give them over willingly."

"Dymorius! Is this…"

"No. But that battle is not far off."

"Your will be done."

The warrior mounted his steed and hastened to his duties. The king again opened the book where the last refrain of its chapter seemed to gleam off its page.

The times of grief have passed
and pain is all forgiven,
Now comes the first and last
to break the crimson ribbon
and sound the trumpet blast.

* * * *

The grey morning dawned with the rhythmic pounding of hooves striding across the foothills. They cut deep into the barren earth under the weight of the exhausted animal, forced onward by an unyielding master. The horse belonged to Dymorius, though he was not its rider. A Batrauk bearing the arm-length scar of a general drove the beast of burden. Arriving at the outpost, the horse stumbling to a halt. The general dismounted and the animal collapsed.

The square wooden building stood on a flat, treeless stretch of land, with frost-laden windows facing the arid hills. Smoke whisked off its chimney, like steam being blown off a cup of hot drink.

He threw open the door, startling the two Batrauks on guard and waking the other three who slept in a pile in the corner. The leader entered with a grunt and slammed the door shut behind him.

"Get up!" he shouted removing his large tin helmet and throwing it onto a table. "I've brought important news."

"Ngraauuk, we're leaving, we're leaving, right?" the brown squealed.

"Oh no, you're staying," he said to the crew of disagreeable subordinates.

"How long?"

"For as long as Dymorius needs you here!"

The others shrieked their complaints with loud wails. "We'll freeze to death!" they said.

"We cannot stay," the brown muttered. "Unless you've brought us more grease and lard."

"Grease and lard, grease and lard!" the tattooed one repeated. Looking at the empty casks along the wall, he kicked them over onto the still groggy sleepers. "You must've been bathing in it every day! You should have a month's supply left to keep you warm!"

"It's been freezing cold this season," one said. "And we expected you to bring the report for us to leave." The others hissed in agreement.

"The kingdom is being threatened. Dymorius

is on his way with forty more. And if you're lucky – there'll be extra lard."

Pulling up a stool next to the fire to warm himself, he explained.

"Two young ones have escaped and are believed to be coming this way. They must be stopped!"

"What's so important about two young ones?"

The leader poked at the fire and its flames rose. "Dymorius wants them, dead or alive. He doesn't care which. He says if they get through, that will be the end of us. All of us!"

"Ngra–ngraauk, if they g-get through, Dymorius will destroy us?" a green asked.

"Yes! We will be destroyed!" Spit flew in all directions as he shook his head in anger, the fire's orange glow reflecting in his watery eyes. "Existence as we know it will be over!"

The room became quiet as the dull guards grasped the seriousness of their situation. The fire popped and crackled and the wind whistled through the rafters and rattled the metal shed outside.

A subordinate, green Batrauk broke the silence. "This man we have locked in the shed then, he really is sent here by Dymorius to capture them?"

The leader turned and looked at them puzzled. "You have a man locked up here?" The veins in his head began to bulge.

"Yes. Ngraauuk, He arrived yesterday claiming to be sent by Dymorius to capture the two who escaped."

Perplexed, he rose to his feet and paced back and forth, his weak mind struggling to put the pieces together.

"It's a trick. He must be trying to get them across," he said. "Bring the man out for interrogation. The young ones must be close at hand."

Six Batrauks squealed and squawked with excitement anticipating the torture.

* * * *

Sleep had been hard to find and Jarrett rose early. He crawled out from under the tarp and stretched the stiffness out of his joints. The wind still gusted, so he dug in the sand of the embankment, carving out an area where he could light a small fire and heat a tin of water. When it began boiling, he added some herbs and spice from his pack and poured it into three cups.

No sooner had he finished making the tea, than Chanse came out from their shelter. Jarrett handed him a cup and he took a sip of the hot liquid. His eyebrows raised and he blinked several times. *Good*, Jarrett thought. *He'll need the extra energy*.

"You'd better wake your sister." Jarrett put Chelly's tea down and began packing their things.

Chanse grabbed hold of the tarp and gave it a shake; nothing stirred. He shook it harder, still nothing.

"Come on, get up."

"Just pull the tarp off of her. I've got to pack it anyway," Jarrett said, putting away the tin and flint. He tied the pack tight and tossed it aside, then grabbed another, all the while considering how they would get past Larshal, the guard post, and into the mountains before nightfall.

Chanse stumbled back into him.

"Careful." Jarrett turned and saw Chanse holding the tarp in one hand and pointing at the empty space with the other.

"What?"

"She's gone. Hey, Chell…!"

Jarrett put his hand over Chanse's mouth.

"Do you want all of Gehenna to know we're here?" he whispered.

Chanse shook his head and Jarrett took his hand away, looking around in the sand for clues as to what might have happened to her.

"There was no struggle. Just her tracks leading away." Jarrett paused. "Pack up our things, will you? I'll see where she went."

Jarrett followed the dry bed until he disappeared behind a bend in the ravine. He found Chelly sitting in an embankment, nestled in her cloak and engrossed in her book.

"What are you doing here?"

Chelly looked up at him in surprise, as if he caught her doing something immoral.

"Oh! I'm sorry. I couldn't sleep, so when it was light enough outside, I got up. I – I just wanted to read my book." Her voice trailed off into a thin whisper.

Jarrett looked at the book in her hand, astonished and a bit perplexed.

"So, you can read."

"Yes, I learned before we were sent into the mines."

"That isn't one of Elder's; he only has scrolls."

"No. It's mine." Chelly closed the book, put it back into her pouch, and tied it shut.

"What's it about?"

Chelly didn't speak.

"I see. It is one of the forbidden books then."

Her eyes widened.

"It shouldn't surprise me. If you two are the fulfillment of prophecy, then why wouldn't you have something as dangerous as that?"

Chelly leaned forward, shoved her hands under her arms, and turned away.

"Don't be afraid. Your secret is safe with me." Jarrett sat down and peered up at the flat grey sky. "I still can't believe it though. There have always been rumors that some survived the burnings, but as the years went on, rumors turned into tales, then tales themselves became half-truths. Most now doubt any ever existed." He looked over at her. "You've read it then?"

"Parts." She nodded, then explained how Elder had revealed some of the book's meaning and mystery. "It's changing the way I understand things. It gives me hope and yet…" She looked at her pouch. "Parts of it have me completely confused, kind of frustrated."

"I should think so.," Jarrett said. "A book like that would not be fathomed by a casual reading."

The sound of heavy footsteps approached and they froze. Chelly's eyes widened and her body grew tense. "Larshal," she whispered.

Jarrett held a finger up to his lips, and with his other hand motioned for her to stay still. Creeping around the bend, he disappeared.

Chelly sprung to her feet, crouched and ready to flee in a moment's notice. She heard a commotion, then Jarrett reappeared with Chanse laden with all three packs.

"When you didn't come back, I followed you," Chanse said.

"I apologize. Your sister and I were talking." He grabbed two of the packs and handed the lighter one over to Chelly. Chanse also gave her a tin of the drink Jarrett had prepared earlier. It was no longer steaming, but she drank it anyway without complaint.

"We should get going," Jarrett said. "With any luck, this dry riverbed will lead us into the mountain and keep us low and out of sight."

They trekked along the ravine that etched itself into the earth, like a long scar cutting its way from the mountains down through the arid hills. After a while, they came to a point where Jarrett stopped and told them to wait. He then climbed the bank to look for signs of Batrauks.

He returned rubbing the back of his neck and pacing. "This is bad," he said. "This riverbed leads us right up to the guard's outpost."

"Can't we climb out and find a different way?" Chanse asked.

"We'd be spotted right away. To get out of it we'd either have to climb over one of those big hills while in plain sight or spend another day walking back the way we came to make our way around to the other side. We just don't have time as a luxury." He paused, rubbing his hand over his unshaven chin. "If you have to…how fast can you run?"

Thirteen

The Rescue

The door to the shed swung open and struck the metal wall with a bang. Larshal woke, though he wasn't sure if he had been asleep or just unconscious. Two Batrauks rushed in and convinced him to move by kicking his half-frozen body.

"Get up!" they screamed, "You're coming with us."

Larshal tried to rise, his stiff body screaming at him with every effort. Portions of his clothing and hair had frozen to the floor where he lay. The attempt was too slow for his captors, however, and the impatient Batrauks grabbed his arms and jerked him up, leaving chunks of shirt and scalp stuck to the floor. His legs remained curled up beneath him, unable to straighten. They banged him around and forced him out through the doorway where the other four waited outside.

The chill of the whipping wind stung every exposed part of his body as they threw Larshal to the ground demanding that he stand. With all his will, he managed to get on his feet, but could not straighten up. The Batrauks circled him in and began their accusations.

"Where have you hidden them?" they demanded, shoving him back and forth from one Batrauk to the next.

Every shove felt like a sledgehammer against his body. It was all he could do to keep from falling to the ground; he couldn't imagine what they'd do if that happened. When he didn't answer their questions, they tore off his tattered shirt leaving him defenseless against the cold, bitter wind.

His teeth chattered. "I don't know where they are."

"Not acceptable," hissed the leader as the others slapped him with their greasy hands, "Dymorius will be here tomorrow with forty more of us and then you will feel like talking."

Larshal hung his head in agony. When he lifted it again, the fist of a tattooed arm felled him to the ground.

* * * *

Jarrett and the twins kept low beneath the cover of the river bank as they approached the outpost. The cold could work in their favor if it kept the Batrauks inside. However, if they were on patrol, or even meandering about the grounds, their cover could be compromised and it would become a footrace – one he wasn't sure the twins could win.

They moved stealthily as they neared the outpost, aware of the sounds of every swish of grass and gust of wind.

A door slammed, followed by arguing. Jarrett and the twins stopped and hugged the embankment and waited. They looked at him and he saw in their eyes the look of prey before its predator, and he knew they would need more help than he could give. They heard the commotion above turn into a scuffle, and something caught Jarrett's attention that piqued his curiosity. He signaled for the twins to remain while he carefully climbed the bank. Spying over the ridge, he saw what he needed and scuffled back down. Grabbing the pack from his back, he rifled through it as he whispered his directions.

"Continue on. Keep moving along the way we've been taking." He pointed at the mountain without looking up, his eyes still searching through the pack.

"See where the tree line begins on the mountainside?" he said without waiting for a response. "We'll meet there." Then he reached in and pulled out a leather pouch a little larger than his open hand. "If you don't see me by midday, go on without me."

"But how would we get across the mountains without you to guide us?" Chanse asked.

Jarrett saw fear in Chelly's eyes.

"Listen, I've never been this far myself," Jarrett said, "And I don't know the surest or quickest route. In fact, I don't know any route. But I do know this, you've gotten this far by some miracle, or fate, or something, and you'll get over the same way, with or without me. Our hope lies in the two of you and somehow you will both make it through. I can't explain how I know, but I'm certain of it."

"What do you mean, how can you be so sure?" Chelly asked. The pleading in her voice begged Jarrett to go with them.

"All I can tell you is, I believe that something big is in motion, and the two of you are right in the center of it. Now take the packs and go!" he said, dumping them into Chanse's arms. "I'll wait until you've rounded the bend, but you must hurry!"

Tears rolled down Chelly's cheeks, and he calmed his tone knowing that fear can paralyze as easily as motivate.

"I will catch up to you as soon as I can. Don't be afraid."

Chelly wrapped her arms around him and squeezed. He signaled Chanse to lead her away. Chanse did as he was told, and soon the two were marching off together. Jarrett watched and waited as they rounded the bend. And when he believed the twins were far enough away, he climbed the river bank.

* * * *

All of Larshal's childhood fears resurfaced, and he curled tighter into a ball as they pummeled him. It jogged his memory back into nightmarish images. His mind blurred and his thoughts became detached. He heard the words, "I don't know!" repeating from his lips but wasn't sure what they referred to anymore. Was it concerning the location of the twins, or was he wondering what had possessed him to trust Batrauks?

The words continued out of his mouth as the pictures in his mind flashed back to the mines. There he saw again the brutality, several Batrauks against one helpless victim. He was small then for an eight-year-old, helplessly peering around the corner at an even younger girl receiving the blows. One landed on her so hard that it knocked the life right out of her. Her body spun around and fell to the floor near his feet and she never got up. The blank expression of death staring up at him had haunted him ever since. Each time he remembered her face, the same phrase went through his mind, "I don't know her, I don't know her, I don't know…I don't know." That was the last he ever saw of his little sister.

One of the guards spoke up, "All this is making my grease wear off, I'm getting dry and too cold."

"Lock him back in the shed!" the leader commanded.

Regret now hit Larshal harder than anything the Batrauks had dished out. He had entrusted himself and the welfare of his people to tyrants. For what? Why? Where had it gotten him? Of all the thoughts flickering in his mind, one seemed clear above all else. *If Jarrett is still out there with them, I must keep the Batrauks occupied and give them a chance to escape.*

With all his strength he threw himself between two Batrauks and broke away from the circle. He tried to run but after a few strides tumbled to the ground. His legs were too cold to move. Instead, he broke down in tears, the thing he vowed never to do since his first day in the mines. And until that moment, he had been true to his word. The Batrauks shrieked with fury. Running over, they pounced on him over and over again.

"Stop! Worthless toads."

Stunned by the command, the Batrauks jumped back to see who gave it, then walked away from Larshal leaving him in a crumpled heap of pain.

One eye had swollen shut and the other refused to focus. Wiping his good eye, Larshal regained some vision. Through the blur, he saw Jarrett. He seemed unarmed except for his hands, which were clenched into fists as if ready to strike.

The mix of relief and guilt overwhelmed him, and doubling over in pain, Larshal threw up.

* * * *

The Batrauks surrounded Jarrett. They closed in and shoved him a few times. He did not retaliate.

"What did you say to us?" the tattooed one said.

Jarrett remained silent. They moved in closer and shoved him more, not noticing the lack of fear in his eyes.

"Are you the one trying to escape with the young ones?"

Still no answer and no attempt to protect himself. With each push, Jarrett could see their grease marks staining his cloak. He watched as their demeanor changed. Their eyes bulged and pulsated as they crowded around him preparing to attack with full force. Jarrett still stood, unmoved.

The scarred commander opened his mouth wide enough to swallow Jarrett's face and let out a high-pitched squeal, the signal to the others to begin this execution. Jarrett had waited for this moment. With all of them within reach, he threw what he held clenched in his fists, unleashing a spray of salt. It burned the Batrauk's unprotected flesh like acid, leaving scars wherever it came into contact. He grabbed the commander by the arm with his salt-covered gloves and threw him to the ground where he writhed in pain. The screams echoed through the hills as Batrauks pawed at their skin trying to brush the salt off of their flesh. Some of it had gotten into one's eyes, blinding him and becoming so swollen they burst, leaving the creatures convulsing and unconscious.

One by one, Jarrett dragged each Batrauk to the shed that had held Larshal captive the night before. Scars appeared wherever he touched them and the stench of their flesh filled the air along with their high-pitched squeals.

With the last Batrauk contained, Jarrett locked the door and turned back to where Larshal had been laying, but he was gone. He looked around for a moment confused until a familiar voice strained to speak.

"Thanks."

He saw Larshal leaning against the corner of the guardhouse. Jarrett stepped toward his old friend, whose broken body slid down the side of the building. Jarrett rushed over, shouldered his weight, and dragged him inside.

"I-I-I came out-t here t-to ca-capture you," Larshal stuttered, wrapping a blanket around his shoulders as Jarrett worked the fire. "To take those t-two from you and turn th-them over to Dymorius, s-so why did you save me?"

"We've been friends our whole lives. Since the mines. Remember?" Jarrett added another log. "You would beat me up so the Batrauks would think we were enemies and keep us together?"

A painful smile brushed across Larshal's face, which turned into a grimace.

"You had to really want to stay together, to beat someone up that often," Jarrett said.

"Stop-p it," Larshal smirked. "It hurts worse when I laugh."

Jarrett found the packs Larshal had carried and scrounged enough things together to prepare a hot meal for his ailing friend. While Larshal ate, Jarrett rummaged through supplies looking for clothing.

"What was I thinking?" Larshal dropped his food onto his lap and tipped his head back. "I'm so stupid!"

"Here, try this on." Jarrett handed him a misshapen shirt.

Guilt grabbed his friend and squeezed as if trying to wring every last drop of life out of him. Larshal's eyes moisten, and Jarrett recalled the day they met in the mines when he stood next to the toughest kid he'd ever seen. A Batrauk had just beaten Larshal bloody, trying in vain to break his spirit. But when the beatings ceased to have any effect, the creature landed one last blow that would have cracked most. He fell facedown to the ground, and the Batrauk stomped away in triumph – or so he thought.

Jarrett bent down and rolled him over. Larshal smiled as broad as ever.

"Never let them see you cry," Larshal said. He gave a little chuckle. "No matter what, never let anyone ever see you cry." He lost consciousness, but the smile remained.

Seeing his old friend like this, Jarrett knew that his ego had taken more of a beating than his body ever had.

"What can I do?" Larshal asked. "I could rush back to the village to warn them and help prepare for the armies that will surely make their way to BorBoros." He rubbed his arms to warm himself then stopped. "But if Unwyn has been unable to dissuade an attack, then the armies are probably there already."

He sat in silence Threw his head back and stared at the ceiling. "Think man, think."

"I could use your help getting those two over the mountains."

Larshal looked at him and after a moment, nodded. He stood up using the back of the chair to straighten himself.

"Sit back down before you fall down! If you're going to be of any help, I'll need you better rested than this."

"We don't have time. Dymorius and his troops aren't going to wait around for me to recuperate." Larshal paced the floor loosening the stiffness in his bones. "These cuts and bruises will just have to heal on the way."

With little daylight left, Jarrett and Larshal headed out, checking the shed to make sure it was secure. No sounds came from within.

"Dymorius isn't going to be happy with them," Larshal said as they walked away. "Or with us. So, where are those two hiding?"

"They've started over the mountain."

"You sent them on alone?"

"What choice did we have? I couldn't leave you to die, and I didn't know how the run-in with the Batrauks would end. But I could at least buy them a head start. Besides, they're brave."

Larshal shook his head. "With little or no clue where they're going, or how long it will take to get there, crossing these mountains on the verge of winter is not brave – it's suicide."

Fourteen

Buried Alive

Shelly sat curled up beneath a large fir tree for shelter and looked out over the valley they had just crossed. The wind rushed through the needles above, making them whistle rather than whisper, and the stinging, damp cold numbed her flesh where exposed.

The winter air marched down the mountainside like a pillaging army, stealing any measure of heat the land possessed. She held the bottom of her hood closed and tucked her knees under her arms to keep the cold at bay. Pressing her chin to her chest, she raised her gaze under the shadow of her hood and watched for Jarrett.

Chanse stood several paces down the hill, facing the valley. The wind whipped his cloak around, but for whatever reason, he didn't seem to notice the bitter chill. He had remained quiet while they made their way to the foot of the mountain and now kept his silent vigil.

Time ceased to move as the grey day cast no shadows, and still, there was no sign of their guide.

The book in Chelly's pouch called to her. She pulled it out, folded her sleeves over her hands, careful not to expose them. Rifling the pages of her book, she called over to her brother.

"I'm going to read. Do you want to hear?" she shouted over the wind.

Chanse walked over to his sister, glancing back every few steps watching for Jarrett's approach. "What'd you say?" he asked.

"Would you like me to read to you?"

"Sure," he answered, then took off his pack and sat down next to her without diverting his gaze.

Again, she felt the flicker of life surge through her from the words she read, like the spark of an ever-growing flame. It wasn't just the words, however, that engrossed her; she felt a deeper connection as if the person who wrote this book knew her intimately. Reading it, she came back to the passage that puzzled her. What it said didn't seem at first to go along with the book's message so far, and she found it disturbing.

It doesn't mean that, she said to herself. *It couldn't. That just wouldn't make sense*. She paused, unwilling to move on in the story until she could grasp it.

"Done reading?" Chanse asked.

Chelly rested the book in her lap, disheartened. "I don't get it," she mumbled.

"Don't get what?"

Chelly explained her dilemma with the text.

"Now you know how I feel," he said. "I don't get any of it."

He stared far off; his thoughts just as distant as his gaze.

"I'm sorry," she said, "I guess I thought you felt the same way about this as I do. You don't feel a change?"

"I don't even understand what you mean by 'a change'."

"So, you don't believe it then."

"I didn't say that," he said getting up and putting on his pack. His words seemed short and Chelly felt put off.

"What exactly *do* you believe?" Her tone came out stern and accusing.

"I'll find out."

"What does that mean? Don't you even know what you believe?"

Chanse clenched his lips and turned with his back to the valley, and started walking.

"Where are you going?" she yelled.

"Over!"

"We have to wait for Jarrett!"

"We have to obey him." His answer came out calm and resolute.

Chelly looked at her brother, puzzled and upset at his heartlessness.

"He could be in trouble and we should help," she said. Standing up, she put her book back into the pouch, then picked up her pack and flung it over her shoulder.

"The best way we can help Jarrett is to make it over these mountains."

Chelly ignored her brother and began

stomping down the hill, back the way they came.

"I don't understand everything about these prophecies," he said, raising his voice. "But Jarrett was willing to risk his life to see to it that we made it across. For some reason, it means freedom, not only for us but somehow for them as well."

Chelly stopped.

"Maybe what we do isn't just about us," he said. "Maybe, we're all connected, and what someone does somehow affects everyone in some way."

Chanse's words turned Chelly around and she walked up to him.

"You know," she said, "I keep reading something like that in this book."

"I *heard* it before."

"From who?"

"Dad."

Chelly followed her brother up the mountainside, each step twisting a knot inside her stomach from leaving Jarrett behind. He could never follow them. Any trail they left would either be whisked away by the wind or covered by the dusting of snow that had just begun. Chelly raised her head to see snow suspended from the mountaintops like flags waving from castle towers. The wind grew stronger the higher they climbed. Yet they pushed onward until they came to the top of a ridge from which they hoped to see what lay before them.

Chanse pulled out his compass. Its rust had worn off from his newfound habit of rubbing it between his thumb and forefinger. He opened it and the arrow inside spun dutifully toward their destination.

"We've got to find a marker to our North, to keep from getting turned around," Chanse said, "or we'll wander around until we freeze to death."

They searched the grey horizon. Thick heavy clouds passed between the peaks, carried along by strong gales. Through them, a shadowy figure appeared in the distance, a lone dominant outcropping of rock. It materialized through the haze of blowing snow, growing darker, getting clearer. It resembled a man, hunched over with a heavy burden on his back walking northward.

Chelly pointed, "How's that?"

"Perfect!" He put the compass back into his pouch.

"What should we name it?" she asked.

"Name it? What for?"

"Come on Chanse, our guide should have a name."

Chanse blurted the first thing that came to his mind. "Then let's name it North since that's the direction we're going."

He began to march on, but Chelly hesitated.

"I was thinking Mount Ada…" Her voice cracked as she tried to say their family name. The further away they walked from their home, the harder the ache inside her squeezed. She lifted her head, swallowed hard, and tried again.

"Mount Adaman," she said.

Her brother stopped and turned.

She dropped her head, but still felt his eyes

upon her. The moment lingered, and Chelly held back the tear that pooled up in her eye. She wanted to regain her composure, to stay strong. Their years in the mines had taught her that. Crying wasn't going to change anything or help anyone.

Then she felt an arm across her shoulder pull her in. She never recalled getting a hug from her brother before. The last ones she could remember were from their mother and father, and that had been so long ago. The memory of it was more than she could take. She buried her head in his arms and let her tears flow freely.

Her shoulders shook no matter how hard she tried to stop them. Usually, Chanse would try to distract her before she had even gotten close to crying. Now, however, there was only silence. He just held her as she let go of the sadness that she could no longer ignore. There were no words of comfort; this was no happy ending, just a series of hard choices. Maybe all of life was just hard choices. Or maybe, life was altogether just hard.

Chelly removed her face from Chanse's cloak. Her tears had stopped and some of the squeezing inside of her released.

She took a deep breath. "We should get going."

"Alright."

Looking at the challenge ahead of them, they plotted their course to a place they considered reachable by nightfall.

"The shortest way is to go down into this valley to the next ridge," Chanse told her.

“That’s a lot of climbing. We can get to the same place by following the ridge we’re on.” She said, pointing out the long, narrow line that wound across the horizon like a snake.

“But that’s longer.”

“But it might not take longer,” Chelly said. “It may even be quicker.”

She could tell by the look on his face that he didn’t agree and that he wanted to march straight across to prove her wrong. But he surprised her by consenting and started along the path she had suggested.

As they plodded along one ridge and then another, the bad weather got worse and dark clouds engulfed the peak of Mt. Adaman. Like dark grey fingers, the sinister billows reached around to strangle the mountain, as if the hand of Dymorius himself reached down to hold them in.

They trekked on as heavy snow and ice began pelting them. It found its way into their hoods and stung their cheeks. The wind continued to blow the white spray around so that neither Chanse nor Chelly could see more than a few feet ahead.

“Chanse, we can’t go any further!”

“I know, I know!” he bellowed over the wind.

Finding no shelter except for the lee side of a boulder, they crouched behind it and pulled out the tarp from Jarrett’s pack. The wind tried to rip it out of their hands, but they managed to wrestle the tarp to the ground. Crawling underneath, they tucked the edges under themselves to keep it from blowing away. Chelly squirmed, managing to remove her pack, and settled in. Placing it as a barricade against elements, she rolled onto her side facing Chanse. He had slid his pack up behind his head and used it as a backrest.

The storm grew even stronger and shook the tarp so violently that it cracked like a whip and slapped Chanse in the face.

"Ouch!" he shouted and rolled onto his side facing her. "If we had gone into the valley, it wouldn't be this windy!"

Even in the dim light, she could see the mark the tarp had left. It looked sore and she felt guilty as if she had slapped him herself.

"I'm…sorry."

"Yeah, well you should be!"

"Chanse, I really am sorry."

Her calm answer seemed to cool her brother's wrath as he rubbed his cheek. "It's not your fault. It just hurts, that's all." He slipped out of his pack and pushed it to the edge as she had done.

Chelly scrounged through their provisions for something to eat and found the dried frog meat. Digging deeper she discovered more. And unwrapping the bottom parcel found still more. Then, in a side pocket, she saw the delightful brown treat that Jarrett had brought for their celebration. She decided that since they weren't *safely* into the mountains yet, they should hold off, so she stuffed it back in the pack without mentioning it. She took out the frog, offered it to her brother, and neither complained.

Chelly ignored the wind and cold by

concentrating on their friends Breena, Drake, and Ricker. The prophecies only mentioned two escaping. Did that mean their friends were captured and returned to the mines? Did two of them escape and already fulfill the prophecies? If they had, were she and her brother just some sort of decoy and had served their purpose? Had they been led here and left to die trying to cross the mountains? She just wanted to know so she could stop worrying. She couldn't escape her thoughts. They chased her as relentlessly as Dymorius himself, and though Chanse was with her, somehow she felt very alone.

Though her mind reeled with speculations Chelly's eyes grew heavy and she sank into a dark, restless sleep. Snow fell hard, blanketing the mountains and burying the twins beneath drifts of white until all sign of them vanished.

* * * *

Jarrett and Larshal arrived at the tree line where the twins were to wait. The already accumulating snow eliminated any signs of them.

"They must've gone on," Jarrett said.

"I still can't believe they would try crossing the mountains alone," Larshal said.

"Come on. If they only waited until midday as I told them, they'll be several hours ahead of us."

They ascended the mountain together with Jarrett rushing ahead to scout, then returning to aid Larshal. The bad weather and Larshal's injuries slowed their pace. Halfway up the first peak, the snowstorm hit full force.

"They couldn't have gone very far in this," Larshal said. "We should stop and build a shelter."

"We'll keep moving. If they stopped already, we might just be able to catch up with them."

"Jarrett, we can't even see where we're going!" Larshal shouted above the wind. "We need to stop!"

"We need to find them!" Jarrett said. He felt blind determination driving him beyond his limits, and wanted to obey it.

"We could walk right past them and not even know it!"

Larshal's words hit him like a slap across the face. He stopped and listened for a distant voice, a cry for help, movement, anything. He heard nothing except the wind. He could barely hear Larshal who stood beside him now.

"Jarrett, I need to rest." His voice startled him. "And, so do you."

They took cover in the cleft of a large boulder that had split in two. The halves leaned against each other creating a long, triangular tunnel. Ducking in, they built a small fire, but the wind would sometimes shift and find its way through their shelter with blowing snow. Keeping it lit became their mission. With it, they were able to retain some heat, but it promised to be a long, cold night.

"How are they going to survive this storm?" Larshal asked packing snow against his swollen eye. He was able to open it now, but it was turning a dark purple.

"I don't know." Jarrett wondered if his advice for them to go on without him had been wise and if he had waited too long letting Larshal recover.

"You honestly believe what Elder says about those prophecies?"

Larshal's question disrupted Jarrett's tendency to worry and he was taken a little off guard. He had never shared his beliefs with anyone before and wasn't sure if he could explain it.

"I hope they are, and that I will see our city rebuilt and restored to its former beauty," he said. "I know that other, older prophecies have been fulfilled such as the destruction of our city and our exile in the bog. What reason do I have to doubt their complete fulfillment when they've proven trustworthy so far?"

"I hope you're right, Jarrett, really I do. But to be honest, I just can't see how those two escaping these borders can bring it all about."

Jarrett couldn't escape Larshal's logic, but he also couldn't escape his convictions. Throwing more sticks on the fire, he broke the long pause. "I guess my faith isn't as much about understanding *how*, as much as it is about believing *that* it will happen. Even if this isn't the time, or these two aren't the ones, I still know that one day the fulfillment *will* happen – it has to."

Fifteen

Forty-four Riders

Clouds raced across the early morning sky gleaming red and gold. A polished black boot pulled out of its stirrup, as the rider dismounted his horse. Signs of a struggle dotted the ground and left tracks leading off to a shed, which puzzled him. He walked over and tried the door. Finding it locked, he unsheathed his sword and with one swing the lock fell to the ground. As the door swung open, Dymorius saw the pile of Batrauks with their flesh burned and frozen to the floor. All were dead. He stood glaring at their corpses, rage surging inside of him.

How could this be? he wondered. *Two young ones are not capable of all this!* He slammed the door shut and returned to the others. Stroking his horse's head, he grabbed its reins.

"They've gotten through here," Dymorius told his general. "There is not much time."

The Batrauk looked up toward the mountains. "Winter is here, my Lord. They cannot pass. You have won."

"I must see their frozen corpses before I'm satisfied!" Dymorius insisted. "As long as they live, a chance yet remains." He scanned his army of Batrauks, greased and ready for battle and his stare fell upon three smaller figures on top of the horse at the rear. They were tied at the wrists and slumped against one another on the back of the animal. The wind pulled at the blankets they were wrapped in, uncovering the face of a young girl with large dark eyes.

"We will go after them!" Dymorius said. "If they are dead, fine. But if they are alive somehow, these three will be our bait to draw them out."

"Hail Dymorius!" the Batrauks chanted in unison, and each time Dymorius felt stronger and larger. He mounted his steed and gave the order to move out. His general echoed the command.

"Forward!"

The horses raced toward the mountain, kicking up the dusting of snow that lay across the foothills.

* * * *

It was dark under the tarp. Chanse hadn't remembered falling asleep but now felt well-rested and wide awake. He no longer heard the wind, only the steady breathing of his sister.

His hand touched his pouch and he pulled out the round metal disc. Memories flooded him.

"I want you to have this," his father had said handing him the compass that always sat on the small table by the hearth. "To remind you that there is one way in life that is right, and it isn't the way you'll learn where they're taking you. It's a way of light, not darkness. Can you remember that?"

Chanse nodded.

"You're good. Let this remind you of that. Don't lose it, son."

It had been his birthday present, just like Chelly had been given the book. His father had rolled it up into one of his pant legs, thinking it'd be well hidden for getting it into the mine. They found nothing in the search, but later when he reached for it, it was gone. He had lost it, and since then felt in some measure that he had lost his father's trust. He tried not to dwell on it, for when he did, his father's love slipped away also. Finding this one redeemed those feelings as if Chanse had been given another chance.

I will never let this one go, he said to himself and slid the compass back into his pouch.

"Chelly, are you up?"

Her breathing changed.

"Chelly."

"I'm up. What's the..." she paused, "Chanse, I can't move."

"It's all the snow. We're buried."

She struggled and her breathing became more rapid.

"Don't panic," he laughed. "We're fine."

"But I can't move!" she grunted as she struggled.

"Hold on."

Chanse maneuvered his way closer to Chelly.

"We'll push together. On the count of three."

The snow gave way in large stiff chunks, as they broke out into the morning light. A few clouds were all that remained of the storm that had passed with the night. Chanse shook the snow off of the tarp and packed it away, while his sister pulled out food for a meal. Any fuel for a fire lied buried beneath a couple of feet of snow, so they settled for cold rations once again.

Chelly handed Chanse the frog meat. He looked at it for a moment before putting it in his mouth. He remembered the first meal he had in BorBoros and his first taste of it – warm and crispy. Cold, the flesh took on a greasy texture that left a coating on the roof of his mouth. He took a bite, ignoring his hunger for something else, and continued to eat until his stomach stopped groaning.

Finished packing, Chanse looked out across the mountains and saw Mt. Adaman, its hunched figure pointing the way.

"That valley down below looks like it would lead us all the way there. It's a natural route to follow, one where we won't get turned around or lost," he said studying their position. "The only thing is..."

"Is getting down there from up here." Chelly finished his sentence. They stood upon a bluff with no clear way down.

"We'll have to keep following this ridge. Hopefully, it slopes down somewhere," Chanse said and started trudging through the snow.

All-day they climbed steadily higher, as the

thinning air left them panting harder with each step. The cloaks that had kept them dry and warm through the valley were no match for the frigid temperatures, and only by constantly moving were they able to keep any warmth. At night they once again huddled beneath the tarp that they buried under a blanket of snow for insulation.

The next morning, Mount Adaman stood in the distance only a day's journey off if they could descend into the valley. But, the bluffs they followed had now become cliffs of hundreds of feet above the valley floor and Chanse saw no signs of them sloping.

They packed their things and tried walking through the now crusty snow. Heated from the sun, and buffeted by an arctic wind, it turned into a sheet of thin ice. If he was careful and moved slowly enough, Chanse found he could stay on top without breaking through, but it would only last a short distance before he would sink again up to his knees. Each time he felt the icy sharp edge break across his leg.

"This snow is hard to walk through," Chelly said.

"Just step where I step," he told her. His shins felt raw and stung as he stamped out his frustration on the trail he blazed.

"Chanse, stop a minute," Chelly said but he ignored her stamping harder as if to punish the snow for being there.

"Chanse!"

"What?" He finally stood still and threw his

head back.

"I think you're bleeding."

He looked down. A small, bright red trail dotted his steps.

"Come on," she said pulling him away from their path to the edge of a cliff where the bright sun melted the snow and left a few clear patches.

He sat on a dry outcropping of rock to examine his leg and felt the warm sun on his skin.

"Are you okay?" Chelly asked, not daring to go so close to the edge.

"Yes," he said wiping off blood to see how deep the wound was. He then took clean snow and held it against his shin hoping to stop the bleeding. It didn't work. "Is anything ever easy?" He threw the now pink ball of snow out over the valley.

"In my book, I've read that the struggles we face can actually be used for our benefit if we believe. That they produce …"

Her voice faded into the background as Chanse made more snowballs and threw them. Watching them drop, he noticed a strange shaggy-looking animal halfway up the face of the cliff. It walked effortlessly along a series of crisscrossing ledges that etched their way up the rocky face from the canyon floor.

The more he examined them, the more it resembled a maze, one he felt certain he could solve. His eyes darted back and forth, up and down, from one dead-end to another. Then he saw it.

This is possible, he realized, and without hesitation lowered himself over the edge.

"What are you doing?" Chelly yelled as he disappeared.

He looked up and saw his sister's fingers and eyes inching over the rocky outcropping.

"Check it out! We can climb down," he said standing on a narrow shelf, "What did you think?" He took several steps and with each step felt more confident about his decision. "This isn't going to be that bad." He looked back, but Chelly wasn't there. She still hadn't stepped onto the ledge. He stopped. "What are you waiting for?"

"Ohhh!" she growled and lowered herself to the path he was taking.

"See it's not bad," he reassured.

She let out a short scream and froze.

"What's wrong?"

"This pack wants to push me off of the wall!"

He turned and could see her legs shaking.

"Put your shoulder to the wall, not your back," he said. "Like this. And don't look any further down than the ledge we're on." He watched her turn and waited as she inched her way toward him.

"How are you doing?" he asked.

"I don't know if this is a good idea," she said, the tone of her voice as shaky as her legs.

Chanse maneuvered his way behind a spiny, waist-high shrub that had sunk its roots into the rocky crags. He clung close to the wall, but its branches still clawed at his pants, scratched his legs, and grabbed his pack. He stomped at them, clearing a way, then waited on the other side for Chelly to push her way through the bramble.

Each ledge offered a challenge of its own. Some would lead straight to the next, while others led nowhere at all. More than once they turned around looking for an alternate route because they had come to a dead end. With several ledges behind them, their pathway began to widen, but more shrubs grew. Stopping, Chanse turned around to see his sister lagging.

"Need help?" he shouted back to her.

"Just because I'm not as fast as you…" she mumbled, climbing her way through another shrub. "Just don't rush me!"

"Not a problem, I'll wait."

Chanse felt good about the progress they were making and didn't see the need to hurry. The sun shone warm against the face of the cliff. Melting snow trickled in little streams past him on their way to a valley far below. For the first time, he felt the weight of Dymorius' pursuit left behind. The only thing they had to overcome now was the mountain itself.

"I'm almost there!" Chelly said.

"Alright." No sooner had he said it than beneath him the ledge gave way and the world around him whirled. By instinct, his arms reached out for anything to grab onto. Time moved in pieces. Images of rock, then sky, then ground, then sky again were all caught in glimpses that blurred into a stream of color. Soon all retreated into a black tunnel. Sight, touch, and sound ceased as everything spun out of existence.

A sudden jerk brought him back to the cliff.

He looked down and saw his feet dangling out over a valley floor still hundreds of feet below. Debris from the ledge he'd been standing on continued its rapid descent, crashing to the canyon floor, where he had expected to be.

"Chanse!" Chelly screamed.

His pack had tangled with one of the bushes that he had hated with such passion on their decent until now, grateful beyond measure for the one that held him.

"I could use a hand!"

"I'm coming!" she yelled back.

Chanse examined his situation, careful not to compromise his position with too much movement. The branches seem strong enough, as he grabbed onto one in case his pack should give way.

"Here, grab my hand," Chelly said, stretching out her arm from a place directly above.

He reached up, but they were still over a foot apart.

"Wait," she said. "I'll lie down." Their fingers touched. "Can you reach higher?"

"I'm trying."

Chanse used the branch to hoist himself up as high as he could and saw his sister leaning out further. They grasped hands and Chanse began shimmying up as Chelly pulled. But with the pack still caught, the spiny limbs held him back.

"Come on!" Chelly's grip on his hand tightened as she pulled with a strength that surprised him. A shower of earth pelted him as the ledge beneath his sister gave way. Chanse fell backward as

Chelly plunged headlong into him. The two swung and bounced, suspended from his pack. Then, one branch after the other cracked and gave way.

* * * *

Dymorius stopped his army in a clearing overlooking a valley. He dismounted and pulled out his spyglass. The brass felt cold against his skin as he scanned the horizon.

He had been defeated trying to pick up their trail, with the fresh snow making it impossible. Resorting to meandering across the mountainside, he stopped at every vantage point and searched for signs of them. So far he had only seen the occasional deer or mountain goat, nothing useful.

Something across the valley, on the cliffs at the other side, caught his attention. He focused the glass, expecting to see another goat scampering among the rocky ledges. To his pleasant surprise, he saw two cloaked figures struggling to make their way down. Dymorius' grin pushed up the corners of his thin mustache. Lowering his scope, he declared, "The fates are with us this day!"

"You have found them, our Lord?" his general asked.

"Yes, they are within reach. And alone." The scope retracted in his hand. "There is a place in the valley, a narrow pass where we can cut them off. If they get down from that ridge alive, it will have been for nothing." Then he walked back to where the three captives were sitting upon the last horse.

"Soon you'll be reunited with your friends, does that make you happy?"

The one in front with the tattered blanket across his shoulders looked toward the cliffs. Dymorius smiled seeing hope in the young man, he would now easily be broken.

"You're the one named Drake, aren't you? I'm afraid it doesn't look like they'll make it. But then treachery is the reward for disobedience."

The boy turned and spit in the ruler's face. Dymorius pulled him from the horse, throwing him to the ground face-first in the dirt and snow.

"I suppose you think you're brave," he said, circling him as he spoke. But the battered pile of flesh on the ground didn't speak or move. "I suppose you thought that was heroic!" Dymorius wiped the spit from his face and kicked the boy. The Batrauks began to squeal. "Well, let me tell you something, hero. Even if the prophecy is fulfilled, it only mentions two crossing these borders, so you'll be extinct either way." The boy muttered something but Dymorius couldn't make it out. "What's that?" Dymorius spun around and picked him up by the hair.

"I don't care what happens to me." The grimace on his face revealed not only his pain but his anger as well.

Dymorius looked back at the other two and saw Breena's eyes moist with tears, then walked over to her.

"It hurts you to see him suffer?" he asked. She didn't answer; she didn't need to.

"Yes, I suppose it would. From what I understand if it weren't for you, he would've gotten away back in the cave. So, in a way his predicament is all your fault, isn't it?"

"Leave her alone!" Drake shouted, but Dymorius just smiled and continued to watch the girl. She swallowed hard and the tears dropped from her cheeks to her quivering chin. Her hair fell, covering her face as she hung her head. He had waited for this sign. Dymorius walked back over to Drake, who had risen to his knees in the snow. Grabbing a fist-full of hair, Dymorius yanked his head back to look at him, then bent down and in the slightest whisper growled, "Don't expect her to live long. I will surely do her in before you."

Dymorius ordered two Batrauks to dismount and to put the rebel back on the horse with the other two. "He may still prove useful," he said. "And check the cords of this tethered dog," he pointed at Ricker who had been straining against his bonds. "He's either about to break free or strangle himself."

The train of forty-four riders descended into the valley, where a narrow passage through a thickly wooded basin offered them both cover and a vantage point. A clearing in the midst of it offered the perfect spot to surround any who passed through.

"From here," Dymorius said dismounting his steed. "There is no chance of them escaping."

Sixteen

The Fall

Chelly clutched onto Chanse, as one by one the branches that held them bent and broke. Her grasp tightened as he reached for the rock face, his hands feeling for any nook or cranny to hold onto. As his fingertips latched around an outcropping of stone, the last branch bent low. His three fingers cupped the hold and the limb snapped. For a second they breathed a sigh of relief, but then the rock Chanse clung to broke away.

Chelly thought it strange in that moment, with the end of her life inevitable, how time seemed to pause. Images of her life in the mine and the torture they endured appeared before her like torn pages from a story she had only dreamt of. Finding the way out and the chase on horseback, almost drowning and getting eaten by a serpent, they all rushed into her mind in an instant of eternity – then all fear disappeared. The sensation of falling cradled her and she felt a sense of peace. *So, this is how it ends* she thought, accepting her fate with such calm that she almost felt relieved.

A sharp tug against her pack snapped her from the daze and almost away from her brother who now hung onto her with great ferocity.

She and Chanse swung like a pendulum over what should have been their gravesite. Even the rocks below could have been mistaken for upheaved tombstones cluttering a long-forgotten burial ground.

"Hang on!" a familiar voice said as they collided hard against the cliff and spun, heading in the opposite direction.

Looking up, she stared into the face of their rescuer.

"Jarret!" Chelly reached around his chest and squeezed as they crashed against the other side.

"How'd you find us?" Chanse asked grabbing ahold of Jarrett's cloak.

"We'll talk when we're safe," Jarrett said. "Chanse can you reach the rope around my waist?"

"I think so."

"Chelly, get your arms around my neck and shoulders where you can get a firm grip."

She reached up and noticed a figure standing at the top of the cliff. "Larshal!" she cried, clinging hard to Jarrett, her grip tightening around his neck.

"Stp – cn't breethh." His words came out in small chunks of air.

Chelly could imagine Larshal pulling out a knife and sawing through each strand.

"Listen," Jarrett said when one of the three-cords snapped and they dropped about a foot.

She looked up; Larshal had disappeared, undoubtedly cutting their lifeline.

Jarrett reached for the ledge they swung toward. His fingers touched, but he couldn't hold on. Swinging back the other way, they dropped again as the second cord snapped.

"Let go of me and grab the rope," Jarrett insisted.

Chelly didn't want to, but she released her grip around Jarrett's neck and grabbed onto the one thing she knew couldn't save her.

Jarrett stretched the entire length of his body, reaching for the ledge. Just as his hands secured their grip, the rope went slack and dropped past them. Slamming against the wall, Chanse fell away but jerked to a stop entangled in the rope several feet below Jarrett. Chelly had coiled it around her leg and arm several times, enabling her to stay close to him even as they bounced hard against the cliff.

"Chanse!" Jarrett shouted. "Can you lower yourself to the ledge below us?"

"If I can get out of this mess."

"Chelly, can you climb up over me to the ledge?" Jarrett asked, his voice straining. Chelly saw the rope digging into his ribs and the shaking of his arms.

She scaled his body and reached the ledge. Her arms trembled as she tried to pull herself up without pushing down on Jarrett. With one elbow on top of the ridge, she searched for a foothold.

A strong hand took her by the arm and lifted her to safety. Larshal stood beside her. He didn't speak, but leaned over and pulled Jarrett up, then took the rope and hauled Chanse up also. Chelly recoiled with her brother, confused as to what would happen now that Larshal had caught up with them all. Jarrett sat with his back against the rock wall, his arms gnarled across his lap in pain. Larshal knelt next to him exhausted.

"What happened? Where'd you go?" Jarrett asked out of breath, his face and hair drenched with perspiration.

"The rope was rubbing against the rocks and fraying fast. I… I tried lifting it away from the edge but my hands got pinched in between." Larshal showed him the cuts that went deep into his flesh. "I knew I had to get down to you as soon as possible. I'm just glad you grabbed on when you did."

"I thought you'd left us," Jarrett said between gasps. "I shouldn't have doubted you."

Larshal shrugged. "I've given you reason for doubt."

Chelly and Chanse stared at Larshal, mystified.

"Would one of you please explain this?" Chanse said pointing at the two fishing partners.

Jarrett told the story of what had happened, from saving Larshal from the Batrauks to finding their trail.

"We followed your tracks to the top of the ridge where they disappeared over the edge. We saw you climbing down when Chanse fell into the bush. Before I knew it, Larshal was taking several lengths of rope from his pack and tying them together, then to me. He then began lowering me to you. When we saw *you* fall onto your brother," he said looking at

Chelly and rubbing his arms. “Larshal dropped me down to your level over there. Where I stood out from the wall and ran along it to get to you. Luckily, I got there when I did.”

Jarrett untied the rope that had dug deep into his sides. He wrapped his arms across his ribs and slumped over.

Chelly found herself staring at Jarrett, his face unshaven and rugged, his eyes intense yet kind. He had risked everything for them, leaving his village and friends, to lead her and her brother to a place he’d never been before with no guarantee of success. There had been nothing in the prophecy of a third person escaping. Still, he protected them, risking his life to do so.

Chanse reached under his cloak and grabbed hold of a ragged part of his shirt. Ripping it off into two strips, he handed them to Larshal.

“For your cuts.”

“Thanks.” Larshal smiled, then grimaced as he wrapped the wounds with the bandages.

Chelly watched the man who had condemned her brother and her in front of the entire village, who had hunted them down to hand them over to Dymorius, and wondered why she should ever trust him. The thought of pushing him off the ledge flashed before her, and in that moment, she imagined him tumbling down to his death. She shuddered. It frightened her to think such a thought could ever enter her mind.

Jarrett bumped her as he rubbed his ribs and winced. Her body ached too. She had little strength left and couldn't imagine another day of surviving in the mountains. Mount Adaman stood before them within reach, but she didn't care anymore. She pulled her knees in tight to her chest and rested her arms across them, then closed her eyes and buried her head.

"It'll be fine; we'll be down soon." Chanse put an arm around her.

"I want to go home," she said, quiet but firm. "And I want Mother and Father there." She turned her face toward him. "I want to be in our house again. I want the Batrauks gone. I want Dymorius gone!" Her voice rose with each demand. "This isn't working, Chanse! I want to go home!"

He took his arm down from around her shoulder and looked away. "There is no home for us. And I'm pretty sure..." He hesitated.

"What?" Chelly said, the word coming out short and fast. She gave him a stern look, but Chanse refused to speak. "What?" she asked again louder. Her brother shrunk back. "Say it!" she demanded.

"Nothing."

"Um, we should…" Jarrett started, but Larshal cleared his throat and shook his head.

"Just say it! You think they're dead, don't you?" Her eyes moistened and she hit him in the arm.

"They're my parents too!" he shouted. "And I want to be with them every bit as much as you. I wish I could have the years back that were stolen from us. I want to go home again, to see them. I want Dymorius and every stinking Batrauk to pay for what they did to us…to everyone!" He took a breath and lowered his voice. "And you're right, things aren't working...but what can we do about it?"

The air fell silent. Melting snow trickling down beside Chelly, soaking her leg, but she didn't move; she didn't care.

"It's not fair." Her voice came out in a faint whisper.

"Fair?" Chanse scoffed. "It's *too* fair!"

Every eye looked at Chanse for an explanation as Chelly shook her head. "You're not making any sense."

"Look, we were all born into this – this one cage. We all have the same dictator, had to grow up in the same mine, by the same rules, with the same punishments. We've all been twisted until we think the same, fear the same, hate the same, live the same, and die the same. How much more *fair* can you get?"

The words he spoke did not comfort her, and she felt angry with him for saying them.

"Then what are we doing this for?" she cried.

"Because I'm sick of fair! I want more than fair, I want to be *free*!" He clenched his hand into a fist and hit the rock wall behind him. "So even though we didn't get to choose being born, or our years as slaves, we are going to choose to get out, to get free, even if it only lasts one hour. If Dad and Mom could have known that we would have this chance, they would have wanted us to take it. They would have even given their lives to help us."

"They did," Chelly said.

"Maybe that's why it was so important to them to tell us who we are, and why you should remember who *you* are, Rachel Adaman."

Hearing her name, and that of their mother's sent a chill down Chelly's spine. He never called her that.

"Wait!" Larshal interrupted. "You have a last name? And you know what it is?"

"Yes," Chelly's said, surprised by Larshal's reaction.

His mouth hung open as if to speak, but no words came out.

"We've never met anyone that had one of those before," Jarrett stuttered, stumbling over his words as if he couldn't believe what he was saying.

"It's no big deal to have a second name."

"No big…?" Larshal started, but the words ceased and he rolled his eyes.

"It's huge," Jarrett said. "Remembering our ancient city gives us an identity of who we are as a people, a group. But you have a family name. You have an identity of who you are as a person, as an individual, as well who you come from."

A part of the ledge broke off under Larshal's foot. "Listen, I know everyone here is exhausted. And as much as I want to, I don't think we can spend the night on this ledge. So, I think the best thing for everyone is to get down from here as soon as possible." Another piece broke. "Without falling."

Jarrett gathered up the rope, and giving some to Chelly, handed the rest to Chanse.

"Here, tie yourself in," he told him. "And pass it back to Larshal."

Chelly fidgeted with her end. "I'm not very

good with knots," she said to Jarrett as he stepped in front of her.

"First, put it around like this."

Chelly lifted her arms and Jarrett reached around her waist, gathering it up. The rope pulled her pouch into her side and the book crushed against her. She slid it out from under the rope as Jarrett snugged it up.

"There we have it, with plenty left for me."

Jarrett tethered himself into the line. It took all day, but by late afternoon they had reached the bottom. Shadows from the mountains already crept into the narrow valley. Finding a place where the sun streamed between two peaks onto a hillside, everyone sat down to rest, and Jarrett scoured the packs for something to eat.

"How much do we have?" Larshal asked. "I'm starving."

Jarrett shook his head. "Not much. Just enough for one or two meals."

Chelly's appetite seemed non-existent, but she took what he handed her anyway and nibbled on it while she cracked open her book. It had been gnawing at her mind and she craved its message as ravenously as the others did food. She skipped the section she took issue with and moved on to a part of the story that she had never read.

Again, it filled her with awe and wonder, and somehow, she felt connected with the stranger who wrote this fantastic tale. She felt as if she knew the writer through the words he'd written. They seemed so profound and yet so simple, so harsh and yet so loving. They explained so much, but then created so much mystery. She loved it.

"Come on, this is no place to camp for the night," Jarrett's words woke her. She hadn't even realized she had fallen asleep and only a few hours of daylight remained in this deep valley.

"Where are we going?" she asked her brother who tied down a pack and threw it over his shoulder.

"Not sure, but they want to see if there's more shelter around the bend up ahead, in case the winds pick up and another storm should come."

Chelly looked around for her pack, but Jarrett and Larshal had it along with everything else.

"What should I take?" she asked looking for anything missing.

"Just yourself," Jarrett said. He led the way through the valley with Chanse marching alongside. She hadn't noticed before, but her brother looked stronger somehow, his shoulders were broader and he kept pace with the two men. For the first time, she saw he was a young man.

The four of them trekked on in silence through the valley. Chelly stayed a few steps behind the others, deep in thought about all she had read in the book when she noticed a shadow walking beside her. She looked up and saw Larshal.

"I noticed you were reading that book earlier," he started. "It seems to be pretty important."

Chelly nodded.

"So…where'd you get it?"

She looked at him cautiously. "My mother."

"I had a mom once," Larshal said, then

laughed at himself. “I guess everyone had a mom once. Can’t be born otherwise”

Chelly just stared at him.

He shook his head. “I mean, it must’ve been important to your mom too, because she wanted you to have it.”

Chelly nodded in agreement.

“The man who fathered me never gave me anything but a whoopin’, but my mom did. Before I was taken away, she gave me this.” He pulled from around his neck a braided leather cord, with its end knotted around a lock of hair. A few inches long and lighter in color than his own, it curled gracefully at the end. “I carry this little piece of her around with me everywhere I go.”

“It’s beautiful,” Chelly admired, wishing she had a piece of her mother to hold.

“She was a great lady.” Larshal tucked it back in his shirt. “A *great* lady.”

He stopped talking, and for a moment, she caught a glimpse of him as someone not so different from herself.

“Let’s camp here tonight. The air is still. We can start a fire and sleep around it,” Jarrett said.

Larshal threw off the packs he carried and Chanse did the same, slumping to the ground exhausted. Chelly noticed that they had made it to the foot of Mt. Adaman and pointed it out to her brother.

“We could use a hand here, little man,” Larshal said looking straight at Chanse who hopped up at the challenge and ran over to him.

They wasted no time gathering fuel and

Jarrett went to work with a flint and stone. Before long a small fire warmed them. The sky grew darker as the sun's last rays weakened behind the horizon and the valley was swallowed in shadow. Jarrett passed out food, but still, Chelly felt no appetite. The frog meat that had sustained them so far, made her nauseous. She looked down at the portion he handed her and handed it back.

Whenever Jarrett neared her, Chelly felt embarrassed. More than once he had caught her staring at him. And then there was the episode on the ledge where her emotions spilled out in front of everyone. She wanted to disappear.

"Here." Jarrett held out his hand and in it was the delicious treat he had given them before.

Chelly's eyes widened and she accepted the dark morsel. For a moment she forgot the sick feeling in her stomach.

"You okay?" he asked squatting down next to her.

Chelly nodded and took a bite, a slight smile escaping her lips. "Thank you."

He touched her shoulder and stood to give Chanse his share of the treat. Again, Chanse put the whole piece in his mouth.

"Where'd you get that?" Larshal asked.

"Elder had me bring it."

"Is there any more?"

"Sorry Larshal," Jarrett patted his friend's shoulder. "None for us."

"Aaaah..."

"Here." Chelly broke her piece into three

pieces and handed one each to Jarrett and Larshal.

"No, it wasn't a very big piece to begin with," Jarret said refusing to put out his hand to accept it.

Larshal took the cue and reluctantly refused as well.

"If we don't all have some, it won't taste as good," Chelly forced the pieces into their hands. "Everything tastes better when it's shared."

"Then Larshal and I will share the piece you gave him," Jarrett said giving his back to her.

"Can't say as I've ever believed that, Chelly," Chanse said smacking his lips and wiping his mouth.

"I've never even heard it before," Larshal said, breaking his piece in half and reluctantly handing it to Jarrett, who smiled and put the small piece in his mouth.

"The valley seems to continue around the bend as we hoped," Jarrett said leaning back against a stone. "With any luck, this route will take us right through the mountains."

"Well then," a voice came from the darkness beyond the firelight. "This just isn't your lucky day."

Seventeen

SURRENDER

Jarrett and Larshal jumped to their feet as Dymorius stepped into the firelight. "I believe you have something that rightfully belongs to me – and I would like them back."

Jarrett stepped between Dymorius and the twins. "And you are?" he said unarmed but ready to defend them.

"My face is on every coin in the country, my name on every law and decree. Bow now before your king, hand over the boy and girl, and I may let you live." Dymorius turned his attention to Larshal. "You must be the one Unwyn told me about. I commend you for leading them here to this spot for me as you said you would."

All eyes shot to Larshal, who looked dumbfounded and afraid. "But I…"

"You can put down the façade now. You're the true hero, having saved your entire village from being punished for the sins of John the Elder. In fact," Dymorius casually rested his hand on the hilt of his sword and stepped toward him. "Unwyn was right for once…about you being the smart one. In fact, I'm thinking you should replace him as the delegate for BorBoros. A man who takes initiative and knows what is right deserves the honor. And, Unwyn has become too…" His face scrunched as if tasting something rancid. "Too self-centered. I will leave it up to you as to what to do with him. Now, if you will, bring the two here to me."

Chelly noticed an odd look in Larshal's eyes. He paused for a long time, then pulled out two daggers, one in each hand. Coming from behind, he pressed them against the backs of the twins and prodded them forward.

Jarrett turned around to face them. "Larshal, what are you thinking? You know what this means."

"Step aside, Jarrett."

"No."

Larshal poked the daggers harder into the backs of Chelly and her brother. Chanse winced, Chelly screamed, and Jarrett stepped aside.

"I have to do this," Larshal said driving the twins past Jarrett. "The village will thank me. You will thank me. All of Asher will thank me."

"Jarrett, stop him!" Chelly's plea went unanswered. "We never should have trusted you," she lashed back at Larshal, who urged them forward.

"Here, take them," he said, delivering the twins within Dymorius' reach. "They are yours."

With a conspicuous grin, the ruler waited, as if Chelly and her brother should willingly step up beside him, all the while keeping his eyes fixed on Larshal.

Chelly looked back. Jarrett stood behind her, his eyes also fixed on the traitor handing them over. As the dagger in her back pulled away, Jarrett yanked her back. Larshal threw Chanse behind him and lunged at Dymorius in one fluid motion.

The ruler's sword drew in an instant and Larshal stopped just shy of being pierced in the throat.

"Oh, you silly mortal man. Did you think your little deception would fool me?"

Larshal panted, not moving. Sweat beaded on his brow with the ruler's sword pressing against his flesh. "You'll never get them as long as I'm alive."

Dymorius laughed. "By all means, how do you prefer to die? By the flick of my sword?" His blade grazed across Larshal's neck letting out a small trickle of blood. "No, I think that since you were most likely the one to blame for the mess left at my outpost, my Batrauks should be the ones to exterminate a pest like you."

As if on cue, his legion came out of hiding from behind every tree. Armed and armored, the Batrauks had them surrounded.

Dymorius slowly circled the twins and their would-be rescuers. "All of you suffer from some sort of..." he circled his finger near his temple. "Delusions of grandeur. You," he pointed at Jarrett. "You actually thought you could lead them over the mountain? It's a ten-day journey! And how much food do you have?" You should be thanking me for saving you from the pain of starvation. And you," he singled out Larshal. "A half-whit if ever I saw one.

How did you think you could help?" He continued circling like a wolf striking fear into its prey before the attack.

"And you two," Dymorius came around near Chelly and Chanse. "This whole mess is because of you. Running off and rebelling against the kingdom, giving people false hopes about overthrowing my reign, encouraging my subjects to mutiny! How shall I punish you? What kind of torture would cause you as much pain as you have caused me?"

Three figures tied together and wrapped in blankets were pushed forward. They stumbled out of the darkness next to him. Dymorius pulled one of the blankets off and threw it aside, leaving a young girl shivering in the cold.

"Breena!" Chelly cried. She tried to run to her but Jarrett grabbed her arm and held her back.

Larshal lurched forward, but Dymorius held his sword up across the young girl's throat. "You don't want those two to see their friends killed before their very eyes, do you? What kind of hero would allow that to happen? Not one they tell stories of I'm certain."

Larshal stopped, his teeth clenching, his grip tight around his weapons.

"I am willing to make a deal with you," Dymorius said. "Hand over those two," he pointed at the twins. "And surrender to me. I will let these three live, and we can all go back together."

Jarrett pulled Chelly and Chanse close to his side. "You didn't come here to make deals."

"There's always room for a deal." The ruler

paced before them, fidgeting with his sword as if finding it hard not to stick something with it.

"I don't trust you," Jarrett said.

Dymorius laughed. "Of course you do," he said. "More than you realize." He lifted his blade and stared down the straight edge that pointed directly at Jarrett. "You trust me to follow through with every threat I make. You have complete confidence in me when I say that you will not leave this valley alive if you don't hand them over. Oh, you trust me all right. Your faith in me is stronger than you think. Yes, very, very strong."

Batrauks edged in until they stood shoulder to shoulder, eliminating any gaps and creating an impenetrable wall. The only way out was through Dymorius and his three captives.

Jarrett turned to Chelly and Chanse. "I don't know how you've made it this far, so if you have any more miracles coming your way, now would be a good time to use them."

Chelly clasped her brother's hand. How had they gotten here? And for what? To see her friends murdered in front of her? She was done with it all. She was too tired, too beaten, and too helpless. She felt her grip loosen, and let go of Chanse.

"You know, I have been very patient." Dymorius grabbed Breena by the back of her clothes and again lifted his blade to her neck. "But, this ends now. You have ten seconds left before this one dies."

Chelly looked across at Breena and her heart pounded. "We surrender!" And without any thought of doing so, she stepped forward.

"Yes, we'll go with you," Chanse said joining his sister.

Grabbing their arms, Jarrett pulled them back. "He has no plans of bringing any of us back alive. Don't do this! Some may still escape."

With the fire dying, their friends faded into shadowy figures standing against the dark blue snow.

"We won't let you have them," Jarrett insisted.

"Ten." Dymorius began his countdown.

"Nine."

"Eight."

Chelly strained to see her friends but saw only two standing there. The blanket furthest from Dymorius lay in a bundle on the ground where Ricker had stood, but no one else seemed to notice.

"Seven."

Chanse stepped forward, but Chelly touched his arm and he stopped. He looked at her and she motioned with her eyes at their three friends.

"Six."

"Five."

"Four."

Chelly saw a second blanket lying in the snow where Drake had stood.

"Three. Do you think I'm bluffing?"

"Two." His cold blade drew a trickle of blood from Breena and she squealed. He smiled.

"One."

Eighteen

The King

It had been too long since he stood before his throng of intoxicated worshippers, drinking in their adoration and fear, feeling their wills yielded over and giving him power.

When he first took over Gehenna he craved nothing but worship. He became the center of parades and made grandiose speeches, selling security to his subjects while taking away their freedoms, and they paid him with cheers of praise. But, the day came when the applause faded; the day a young man dared to stand up and protest. He accused Dymorius of deception, of not providing what he'd promised, and even of incompetency to do so.

The atmosphere of adoration quickly changed to confusion and disdain, and for the first time since rising to sovereignty, he felt his power wane.

As they brought the young man before him, Dymorius found that punishment brought fear, and fear also gave him the power he desired. That day his appetite changed. Discipline became punishment, and punishment turned into torture. And, once he tasted torture, it became his delight.

Dymorius turned with a smile toward Breena ready to quench his desire. But, his grin twisted, overtaken by confusion. Her empty wrap hung limp in his grasp, and two more laid vacant in the snow. His three prisoners were gone.

Dymorius dropped the garment and spun around, wielding his sword against an enemy he could not see.

"They're here. I feel their presence." His thoughts muttered involuntarily from his lips, and even with the chill in the air, sweat beaded upon his brow.

"They are watching everything we do. So why do they wait – unless they wait for him?" His smile returned and stretched the corners of his mouth from behind his scraggly mustache. "So, *he* is not here," he said under his breath. With renewed courage, Dymorius shouted to his Batrauks. "Tie the four hand and foot, and prepare a very large funeral pyre!"

They obeyed. Chanse, Chelly, Jarrett, and Larshal were overtaken by the Batrauks and bound together. Soon a swirling blaze rose like a pillar at the foot of the mountain. As the flames lit the valley, the Batrauks squealed out their battle cries and filled the air with their vulgar chants that echoed off the canyon walls.

"Throw them in now?" His general asked.

Dymorius took a deep breath. "Not yet," he

said. "Stoke it hotter."

"B-but it's white-hot now."

"Hotter, hotter! Seven times hotter!" he snapped. Lifting his gaze, he surveyed the hills and shouted to them. "Show yourselves now or these four will surely end up as ashes!"

Two warriors appeared from the shadows. Their bronze armor over white tunics signified their service to another king. The Batrauk's battle cries turned to hisses and croaks of disdain.

"Hold your ground!" Dymorius commanded his troops. "You are about to see the weakness of our enemy."

Calling his general to his side, Dymorius lowered his voice. "The three that were rescued must be near. Find them and bring them to me."

The general stomped off as the Batrauks broke from the circle and surrounded the warriors, who made no attempt to counter. They stood with their backs to each other, swords drawn, unmoved, unlike the Batrauks who swayed back and forth with a nervous rhythm.

"Artheos!" Dymorius shouted. "Do you insult me by sending these two to fight for you? Answer me!" But, only the sound of his voice echoing through the valley returned.

"Just as I thought, he is not here. He merely sent spies."

"Don't you know where you are?" one warrior asked. "You are in the country of Hamar. You hold no fear here."

Dymorius' general approached his master,

"As you wished." He brought forth Drake, Ricker, and Breena.

"Excellent. To show these spies that we are not weak or afraid, I will slay them in front of everyone, then send these spies back to their master with the news. We'll keep the other four alive until we're out of the mountains – as insurance."

The general tugged on the rope that bound his three captives. Breena, Drake, and Ricker stumbled forward.

Dymorius sheathed his sword and pulled out a ritual dagger pressing its wavy blade against Breena's cheek. Her eyes widened in fear. A sudden tug against the rope by Drake jerked her away and she fell, pulling him and Ricker down on top of her.

"What's the matter?" Dymorius smiled standing over them. "Would it pain you to see your pretty little sister become an ugly creature? I wouldn't dream of not having you witness it!" He bent down onto one knee and grabbed Drake by the hair, turning his face toward her.

A violent rumble from the hills interrupted his threat, as an avalanche of twenty-seven warriors on white horses came charging down the mountainside into the valley.

"Now, this is more like it." Dymorius let go of Drake and rose to his feet. Grabbing a nearby Batrauk, he handed over the dagger, "If things get out of hand, I leave it to you to make sure that they do not leave this valley alive. And, if you should fail, do yourself a favor – use the blade to gut yourself."

The Batrauk accepted the dagger and stood

hovering, ready to carry out his duties at the command.

The flames of the funeral pyre rose behind Dymorius, as he turned to face his enemy. He approached them, remembering their training, their unquestioned obedience to their king. *Mindless*, he thought to himself. *They wouldn't hurt a fly unless commanded to.* He stepped boldly before their ranks.

"Which of you would die first?" he asked. "Maybe you?" In one swift movement, Dymorius spun around, drew his sword, and placed the tip on the helmet between a warrior's eyes in one swift movement.

The warrior didn't even blink. He stood firm in his burnished armor gleaming like gold reflecting the fire's glow, and holding his bronze shield polished to a mirror-like finish.

Dymorius let out a small laugh, pulled his weapon back, and smiled. For a moment all was silent, except for the crackle of the bonfire. Then, as if by some unseen, unheard cue, the regiment parted. Their ranks split in two as another rider entered the assembly.

He too, wore white with bronze armor covering his chest and legs. Even his white horse was clad in bronze. He rode to the front of the ranks, dismounted, and stepped face to face with Dymorius.

* * * *

Chanse watched King Artheos as he stood tall

and confident, unafraid of the one who held Gehenna in terror. His eyes, fearsome as a tempest, were framed by a strong brow and angular features. Prominent cheeks rose from his full dark beard, unlike Dymorius' thin mustache, which couldn't conceal the snarl on his lips and made him look like a mangy dog.

"Dymorius, what brings you to the borders of Hamar?" the king asked.

"I don't believe I am yet in Hamar, old friend."

"The borders are clearly marked," King Artheos said, pointing to a series of square stones that dotted the valley pass at least fifty strides beyond the pyre that the Batrauks had built. Chanse wondered how he had not seen them when they came through. Half were covered by snow, but their pattern was unmistakable.

"You know very well what I came after. I came for what is rightfully mine. Or, don't you believe any longer in justice?" Dymorius paused for a reply, but none came. "Don't think you can destroy me just because some runaways made it to your border."

"Your demise doesn't come because of them," he said, "but because of me."

"So, you admit you intend to kill me – friend. That is what you used to call me, isn't it?" Dymorius looked away and shook his head. He then turned back pointed his finger. "See! Your goodness is not as longsuffering as you would have everyone believe."

The king's eyes moistened but no tear fell.

"My heart longs for the one I used to know as a friend, but you are no longer him."

"No, I'm not." Dymorius inched closer, lifting his head before a king who could no more cower before him, as a lion would before a mouse. "I'm wiser and better than that now…and better than you." He stared intently, not shifting his gaze from the king's eyes who returned the stare. "Are you still holding onto your ideals, Artheos?"

Again, the king did not reply.

"And, where have they gotten you so far? Your so-called compassion would even jeopardize the innocent here tonight." Dymorius paced in short strides, and for a moment was silent.

"Can you see Breena or the others?" Chelly whispered as she tightened her grip around Chanse's arm. He craned his neck looking for their friends, but the fire between them blocked his view.

"Yes, this all lands on you, does it not?" Dymorius continued. "You set this all in motion when you granted the power of choice. We could all live in peaceful harmony if you would make all wills subservient to one. But, you won't do that, will you? You prefer to risk suffering and pain, rather than ensure security and equality."

"Is that what you've come to believe?" Artheos asked.

"It's what I know to be true. But, I plan to restore order. When all serve me, they will all, from the least to the greatest, find pleasure in the intoxication of worshipping as one, like it was before you decreed freewill."

Artheos lifted his gaze and caught Chanse's eye, then turned again to Dymorius. "And, when you've dominated and manipulated them into servitude, then where is love?"

"Love? Love is a weakness. Like a diseased cell in a healthy body, love destroys." Dymorius shouldered his weapon, still pacing but more confident. "Is it still not obvious? Can't you see the truth that stands before you? Ultimately, love brings…no, *it demands* death. And, always it's the death of the innocent. So, you may want to put aside your ideals for one night Artheos, and at least this evening consider a deal in order to save them!" He pointed in the direction of Chanse and his sister. "Let me take what is mine – or death will enter your land when I sacrifice them here on your soil."

The king's hand rested on the hilt of his sword. His eyes never veering. His stance sure. "You are in no position to negotiate." King Artheos drew his weapon from its sheath.

Dymorius withdrew. The king didn't move but followed Dymorius with a stern, fixed stare.

"The decision is yours, Artheos," he said, making his way toward them. "Whether they live or die, you decide their fate."

"Chanse, why doesn't he say anything? Is he going to let us die? Where's Breena?" Chelly asked out of the corner of her mouth. Chanse shrugged. Everything happening around him at that moment seemed surreal as if it were pictures from his imagination while being told a tale.

The king's expression still did not change, his

stare dissecting Dymorius like a two-edged sword. As Chanse watched, he could've sworn that Dymorius shrank in size.

"As I said," Artheos scanned his surroundings, thirty warriors against forty Batrauks, then once again locked eyes with Dymorius. "You are in no position to negotiate."

"By all means then, have it your way. But if I kill them, that could hardly be accepted as an escape, and the prophecy would not be fulfilled. But then, are you truly a king of your word?" He stood close enough now for Chanse to see that perspiration covered his face and he looked pasty and pale as if he were feverishly sick.

Chanse squirmed trying to escape but to no avail. Chelly couldn't move either. Even Jarrett and Larshal fought the chords with little or no effect. They were knotted together in such a way that they could not move without wrenching the person next to them.

"The fire, NOW!" Dymorius commanded, raising his blade high in the air for all to see. A dozen Batrauks grabbed Chanse, Chelly, Jarrett, and Larshal and lifting them over their heads, threw them into the flames. As they landed on the mountain of glowing coals, a column of sparks rose into the night sky.

Two Batrauks fell into the inferno with them. Their bodies arched in agony as flames devoured the shrieking creatures. Fire consumed the ropes that bound Chanse and the others, but to their amazement, they did not burn. Their hair, skin, and clothes remained completely unharmed. To them, the fire felt like a warm summer breeze.

Through the flames Chanse watched Dymorius stand frozen with his sword still held above his head. Confusion twisted the expression of triumph off his face, his arm dropped.

King Artheos shouted out his command with a thunderous roar. As it echoed through the mountains, his warriors lifted their shields, blinding the Batrauks with a gleam as bright as day.

Everywhere Chanse looked, Dymorius' army struck out in panic. Many tried to run, only to meet the steel of warrior blades. Others lashed out blindly into the light and slew each other.

Unable to see through the glare of shields and flame, Batrauk fought Batrauk unwittingly. One threw another into the fire. It landed next to Chelly, grabbing her leg as it writhed and squealed from the burning torment. She screamed and kicked it off, backing into Jarrett's arms.

"Come on!" Jarrett grabbed Chelly and leaped out of the fire followed by Larshal.

Chanse was close behind when he looked up and saw through the flames, a Batrauk with a dagger standing over his friends and plunging the blade into them.

"No!" he shouted ready to run out after them, when another Batrauk, thrown onto the pyre, landed on top of him. It knocked him down, pinning him between the burning creature and the hot coals. The more he tried to get up, the more the embers shifted beneath him and the weight of the creature pushed him deeper down into the middle of the fire.

The heat smothered him, making it almost impossible to breathe, and then the weight of yet another Batrauk landed on top. Chanse tried pulling himself out from under their cooking corpses, but the coals were like sand, always settling beneath him. He reached his hand out of the embers to grab hold of anything solid when another hand grabbed hold and pulled him out.

"You alright?" Jarrett helped him to his feet.

"We thought we lost you," Chelly said wrapping her arms around him.

Chanse tried to catch his breath. "Not so tight." He coughed.

"No time for sentiment," Larshal said "We can't stand around here just waiting to be slaughtered. Let's go!"

The battle around them grew frantic. If they tried going left, fighting erupted before them and blocked their way. If they tried right, it sprang up there and became impassable.

"Go around behind the fire. Make your way to the warriors in white!" Jarrett said as he and Larshal held off more Batrauks.

The twins ran behind the pillar of flame, away from the battle. Once out of the war zone, Chelly collapsed in the snow.

"I can't run anymore." She panted. "It's like all my strength is gone."

Chanse laid down beside her, breathless.

"Where are the others?" she asked.

Chanse didn't want to tell his sister what he'd

seen, so he put his arm around her and closed his eyes.

Reaching into his pouch, he pulled out the old compass. He rubbed it between his fingers, rolling it around in his hand. It was smooth now from his habit. The rust was gone and much of its brass finish had tarnished to a dull brown, unlike the gleam his father's had. Still, discovering this one in the cave felt like finding forgiveness.

Chanse opened his eyes just as a large brown Batrauk came running at them. It stood head and shoulders above the others with a general's scar running the length of his arm. He didn't seem phased by the confusion behind him as he lifted his sword and swung it down upon them. With no time to move, Chanse flinched, covering his eyes on reflex.

Nothing happened.

"Get back!" Jarrett, who had deflected the deadly blow, wrestled with the creature and Larshal rushed to his aid. The Batrauk threw Jarrett aside lancing his arm and leaving him writhing in the snow with a gaping wound.

Ignoring the fallen, the Batrauk advanced on Larshal, who reached for his daggers. His hands felt nothing, the blades were not at his side. The general swung his sword at Larshal's head, but Larshal outmaneuvered him landing a fist to the creature's midsection. The Batrauk doubled over, and Larshal pulled off the general's helmet, throwing it down. Raising his arms over his head, he clenched his fists together to bring a monstrous blow down on the creature's head.

"This is for my sister!" he shouted through clenched teeth. But before he could strike, Larshal froze. Pain shot across his face and he doubled over. The Batrauk had thrust his sword through Larshal's inner thigh, piercing a major artery. Larshal fell to the ground, staining the snow bright red with his blood.

The Batrauk got up, his eyes fixed on Chelly as he advanced. Chanse squeezed the compass, pressing it deep into his palm. All the noises of battle dissipated into muffled tones, and time itself moved in pauses. He saw Larshal trying to rise from the ground, and then collapse again. He watched Jarrett rush at the Batrauk, who turned and thrust the sword into his belly, dropping him back to the ground.

Chelly's scream echoed in Chanse's ears, as she bolted toward Jarrett.

Chanse found himself running after her as the Batrauk swung his weapon. Chanse pushed her out of the way. The hilt of the blade hit him, knocking the compass from his hand as he landed on the ground. He rolled to his side as the creature swung again, missing him by a mere hairs-breadth. The near-miss buried the blade in the ground. Chanse scrambled to his feet, but the general grabbed him by the cloak and threw him back down. Yanking his sword from the earth, the Batrauk stood over Chanse and raised the blade above his head with both hands.

In the distance, the battle between Batrauks and warriors filled the valley. Dymorius stood on one side of the fire. He had regained much of his size, soaking in the fear of his Batrauks and Chelly's scream like praise.

King Artheos stood on the other side, his eyes catching Chanse's, directing his gaze toward the stones that lie before him marking the boundary. He and Chelly had passed them when they ran away from the battle. They were no longer out from the rule of Dymorius, they were back in Gehenna!

Nineteen

A Choice

Chanse scurried back on heels and elbows, trying to escape the general's reach, but the Batrauk kept his focus and his gate in step with Chanse's attempt. Backing against a large boulder, his hand landed on something in the snow. He grasped the smooth, round surface of the compass he had dropped and again felt his father's presence.

As the Batrauk's sword drew back, somewhere inside, Chanse heard his father's gentle voice say, "It's ok. You've never disappointed me. Let it go. The compass is not me."

An inner pressure built up like Chanse had never felt before. He raised himself onto his side, gripped the compass tightly, and hurled it with all his might. As the general stepped forward to land his blow, the compass struck him squarely between the eyes. Instead of bouncing off, blood sprayed leaving the object protruding from his general's thin skull.

The Batrauk's body went rigid and his hands lost their grip, dropping the sword to the ground. As his eyes rolled back in his head, he fell to his knees twitching and quivering. The lifeless creature fell face down into the snow.

* * * *

The Dictator looked at his army that had started as forty strong now dwindled to just a few. He ran to his horse and mounted it as one who had just enough strength to hang on. It fled into the night and back to the shadows and safety of his own land.

Artheos faced the dark valley that led to Gehenna, his back to the ending blows of the battle. The sound of fighting stopped with the body of the last slain Batrauk thrown into the fire. A warrior approached the king and stood silently at his side.

"Dymorius is gone," the king said.

"We will pursue and capture him."

"No. Let him go. This is merely the sign of his end. Instead, bring the wounded inside our borders."

Artheos turned to his band of warriors. "Tonight," he said making eye contact with each in turn, "you did very well. I am honored by your courage and faithfulness."

He walked over to where the injured had been placed near the pillar of fire and knelt beside the man who had been stabbed. He had lost a lot of blood and his face had turned the pale color of death. The girl sat at his side pressing her cloak against the wound to stop the flow, but the stab was deep and his blood soaked her garment. Artheos placed his hand upon the man's sweaty brow.

"What is his name?"

"Jarrett...his name is Jarrett." the girl said, keeping her eyes on the wound and trying to control the loss of blood. "Can you do anything for him?" she asked as Jarrett stiffened with pain.

Artheos removed the girl's blood-soaked cloak and touched the man's side; his whole body went limp.

* * * *

Chelly had seen death before in the mines. She'd watched as the body exhaled its last breath, the vacant stare of eyes that would never again see a blue sky or green tree. Those were nameless strangers like herself, unlike the hand she now held in hers.

"Don't give up now, Jarrett. Jarrett?"

His fingers went cold. *How could it be that she and Chanse escaped at the cost of others?*

"It's alright," the king said and tossed her cloak aside.

Chelly looked up at him. "He's gone."

The king lay one hand on the open wound and the other on Chelly's shoulder. It felt strong and full of life, unlike the one she held. He spoke a word that she didn't understand.

"Sodzo."

Warmth rushed from the king's touch, through her body to Jarrett's hand. Chelly looked down at the dead man. His eyes fluttered as he took a deep breath. Color filled his face and a powerful squeeze gripped her fingers.

The king rose to his feet. Jarrett leaned up on his elbows, looked down, and touched his stomach. His hand trembled. There was no more wound. Jarrett stared up at the king.

"Thank you," he said.

The king nodded. "You're welcome." Then he turned and left to assist Chanse with Larshal.

"Y-you're alive." Chelly curled her arms around Jarrett's neck and squeezed.

"Yes, but how?"

Jarrett stood to his feet, unwrapping himself from Chelly's embrace. "I felt the cold, numbing hand of death take me. And then one moment later I was back. How?"

Chanse and Larshal strode up with big grins on their faces. "What just happened?" Larshal threw his hands into the air. "One minute I'm bleeding to death, the next thing I know this king comes over to me, places his hand on my leg, and look!" He slapped his thigh. "No wound! Not even a scratch."

Chanse grabbed Chelly's hand. "Come on," he said and ran with her toward the king.

The closer they came to King Artheos, the more nervous Chelly felt. It seemed strange to be afraid of the one who had delivered them from Dymorius, but this fear felt somehow different – it seemed reasonable.

They stopped a few strides away and waited as the king spoke with one of his warriors. When finished, the warrior left and he turned his attention to them.

"Well now, what can I do for two who have come so far at such great risk?"

Chelly swallowed hard. "We have come for…" Her throat went dry and her words stopped in her throat.

"What she's trying to say is, we have no place to go."

The king knelt in the snow before them. "I have a place specially prepared for you two."

"What do you mean? You knew we were coming?" Chelly asked.

"Of course, I knew the moment you left Tartrus."

"How could you have possibly known that?" Chanse asked.

"I knew you were coming because you answered my call."

"I don't understand," Chelly said. "What do you mean?"

"I don't remember hearing any call," Chanse said, his eyebrows scrunched together.

"You most definitely answered young man, both of you did." He stood up as one of his warriors approached and handed the king a thick blanket. He then wrapped it around Chelly.

"Come walk with me and I'll tell you a story." The king placed a hand on each of their shoulders and led them toward the warmth of the fire.

"Generations ago, there was a young lady who lived in my kingdom. She wrote down everything in diaries. I admired her diligence and treated her with the same attention and respect as everyone else, but she turned against me in the rebellion, though I pleaded with her not to. When I left and Dymorius took over, she had a change of heart, but could not escape the consequences of her decision. Realizing her error, she tried to leave Gehenna, and like many others, was hunted and hid in caves to avoid capture." Artheos stopped walking. "She was executed in one of those caves, and I grieved for her. But, what Dymorius meant for evil was redeemed when you found one of her diaries."

"What do you mean?" Chelly asked.

"Her diary showed you another place to live other than Gehenna. I used her words and many other things to help you on your journey."

"Like what?" Chanse asked.

"When you were pursued through the tunnel, I used the old trap to seal you off from your pursuers. Since you can't swim, I used the monster that swallowed you in the swamp to keep you from drowning." King Artheos laughed. "I even used Larshal's unbelief to hurry you along, so that you'd make it into my boarders before Dymorius could catch you."

"You arranged all of this?"

"I used what each of you chose to do, to bring about the results we all wanted. You wanted to leave; I wanted you to escape. You wanted to find me..." He smiled. "Here I am."

"We heard that you are a good king who is good to your people," Chanse said.

"Many say that I am. And those who know me, trust me to be."

Chelly looked down, feeling inadequate to stand in the presence of a king who held the power of life and death in his hands.

"Don't be afraid," he said, turning her chin toward him. "If you believe that I am as you say, a 'good king', if you trusted me before you even met me..." He looked over to Chanse. "And risked your lives to find me..." His smile broadened and lit his eyes. "Then I am honored to have you live with me in my kingdom." Then he cocked his head as if puzzled, and asked, "But let me ask you something. When you had so many opportunities to give up, why did you keep going?"

Chelly's hand brushed against her pouch. She reached in, pulled out her book, and held it out to him."

"So, you like my book?" King Artheos asked.

"It's my mother's," she said, correcting on impulse.

He smiled.

"Wait. You...you wrote this?" she asked.

He nodded. "And when you read it, you heard my call."

"But Chanse didn't believe your book as I do."

Chanse stepped back. "Well, she didn't start reading it until Elder..."

The king pressed his finger to his lips, silencing them. "Shame is not needed here. The important thing is that you came and that wouldn't have happened without believing in something better."

"The people of BorBoros believe that if we made it out of Gehenna, their village would be set free from the rule of Dymorius. That it would even mean the end of his reign," Chanse said.

Tears welled up in Chelly's eyes, "Breena, Drake, and Ricker believed in something better too, and they died for no reason."

The smile on Artheos' face left. "Knowing the reason doesn't always make things easier. The trick is to take what others meant for evil, and turn it around for something good."

"How can you make something good out of something so pointless?" Chelly asked.

"Pointless is sometimes just a matter of perspective. For example, from your point of view, your friends died. But, from mine…" King Artheos stepped aside. Behind him in the distance stood Drake, Ricker and Breena standing with one of the king's warriors.

Chelly stumbled a few steps forward in disbelief, then stood motionless. She looked across at Breena and caught her stare.

Chanse almost knocked his sister over running past to join their friends. He, Drake, and Ricker tackled each other until they lay in a triumphant pile of joy and laughter, but Chelly couldn't move another inch.

"They were gone. I'm sure of it. Gone," she kept saying. Her legs gave way and she dropped to her knees in the trampled snow. As she buried her head in her hands, a pair of frail arms wrapped tight around her neck.

"You're alive?" Chelly grabbed hold of Breena's arms.

Breena squeezed her hard and laid her head on Chelly's shoulder as she embraced her. Chelly looked up at King Artheos, tears blurring her vision. She blinked them away, but they immediately filled again. She felt the king's strong hand pat her back as he walked past, his laughter mingling with the jubilant shouts of others. Feeling her strength returning, Chelly stood.

"Are you alright?" Breena asked.

"Yeah," she said, her voice breathless. She felt a smile cross her face and the warmth of happiness come over her, that she hadn't felt since she was five.

"We made it Chelly – all of us!" Chanse said gathering their friends around her.

"I don't understand." Chelly looked at King Artheos. "The people of BorBoros said only two would escape, and yet we're all here."

"Yes," he said. "Well, prophecies can be a strange thing and easily misinterpreted, because they give only glimmers and shadows of what will pass. The people of BorBoros have seen only a sliver, the part that concerned them. They knew of only two because they saw only two. Now, if you'll excuse me."

King Artheos walked over to greet Jarrett and Larshal who spoke of rebuilding their once noble city. Amidst the clamor of celebration, Drake asked a question that left them all silent. "What happened back there? Why didn't the fire burn any of you?"

A warrior standing nearby answered them. "Fire has power, and all power here belongs to our king."

"Welcome to Hamar, new citizens!" Artheos' voice echoed as he mounted his horse. "Come as my honored guests and join me for a feast. For your victory this day is the beginning of the end for Gehenna and freedom for its captives!"

The warriors cheered and the others joined in with shouts of victory, as their king led them down the mountain to a place they could call home.

The End...

The great doors to the hall flew open and slammed against the wall. A hunched figure stumbled in, his clothes hung loosely from his thin frame. He limped over to his throne, leaned against it, and slumped onto its seat.

A gnarled figure of a man appeared in the doorway. "My Lord? My Lord! You have returned. If it pleases, the Sorcerer awaits you."

Dymorius glared at him from beneath his sweaty brow. "Come here."

The servant hobbled over to his master.

"Where is he?"

"In his haunt, my Lord."

"Summon him."

The servant shuddered. "B-but my Lord, he does not come out."

Dymorius grabbed the servant by the neck and squeezed.

"Tell him that *he* comes to *me*."

Dymorius released his grip. The servant fell, struggled to his feet, and hurried out of the room gasping for air.

"I rule here." Dymorius clenched his teeth and spit the words at the emptiness around him. The doors slammed shut, and one by one the candles flickered and died, curled trails of smoke rose from their blackened wicks.

"The darkness grows deeper, the shadows, longer." The thin voice of the Sorcerer drifted to his ears from every corner of the room. "Soon it will reach beyond the borders of Gehenna. And your kingdom will rise, as his falls"

"He is stronger. And I have no power there."

A mist appeared, a transparent shadow that materialized at Dymorius' side.

"His strength is his weakness," he whispered. "To take you by force, he must become what you are. To destroy you, he must first destroy himself. And you will prove to be the stronger one. Make him come to you, for you see, he cannot win."

"Yes. He must break his own rules." Dymorius rubbed his hand across his chin.

"And yet his standards do not apply to you, Lord Dymorius."

"Are you certain I will prevail?"

"You will rise to the highest heights. Your throne will far exceed his. All strength belongs to you. For I shall fill you, and combined we shall rule with all power!"

A smile turned up the corners of Dymorius' mouth. "Yes. Come in."

He closed his eyes and took in a deep breath, drawing in the spirit. Regaining his once impressive size, his muscles filled his breastplate until its leather straps stretched and snapped.

"I will prepare a vast army, worthy of my name," he said as a fiery red glow pierced the slits of his eyes.

Made in the USA
Monee, IL
10 March 2021

62431536R00128